THE CORONA YEAR DIARY
OF SIGURD BERGMAN, MD

THE CORONA YEAR DIARY OF SIGURD BERGMAN, MD

A NOVEL

JOSEPH A. BONELLI

SUNSTONE PRESS

SANTA FE

Sunstone books may be purchased for educational, business, or sales promotional use. For information please write: Special Markets Department, Sunstone Press, P.O. Box 2321, Santa Fe, New Mexico 87504-2321.

Book and cover design › R. Ahl
Printed on acid-free paper
∞

eBook 978-1-61139-634-8

———

Library of Congress Cataloging-in-Publication Data

Names: Bonelli, Joseph A., 1942- author.
Title: The Corona year diary of Sigurd Bergman, MD : a novel / by Joseph A. Bonelli.
Description: Santa Fe, NM : Sunstone Press, [2021] | Summary: "A fictional diary of a medical doctor and his reflections on Covid-19"-- Provided by publisher.
Identifiers: LCCN 2021035224 | ISBN 9781632933492 (paperback) | ISBN 9781611396348 (epub)
Subjects: LCSH: COVID-19 Pandemic, 2020---Nevada--Las Vegas--Fiction. | LCGFT: Diary fiction.
Classification: LCC PS3602.O657156 C67 2021 | DDC 813/.6--dc23
LC record available at https://lccn.loc.gov/2021035224

———

WWW.SUNSTONEPRESS.COM
SUNSTONE PRESS / POST OFFICE BOX 2321 / SANTA FE, NM 87504-2321 /USA
(505) 988-4418 / FAX (505) 988-1025

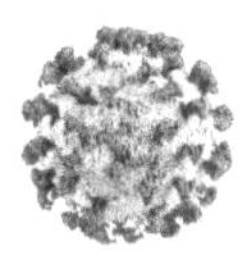
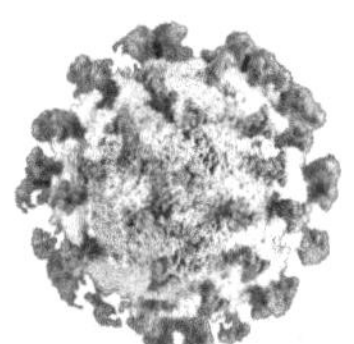
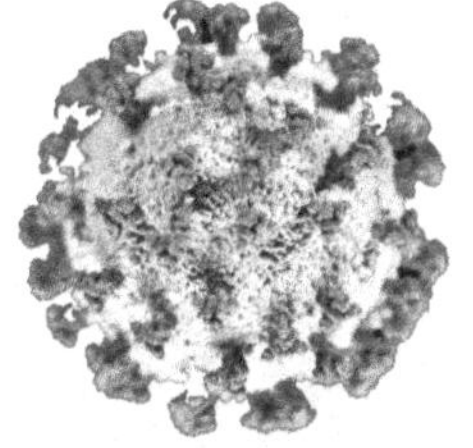
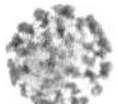
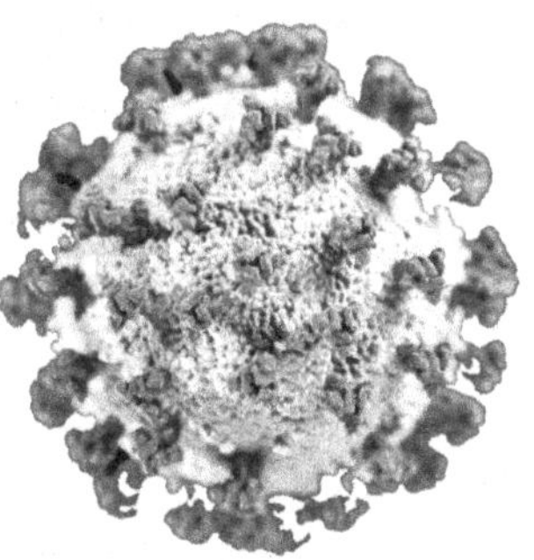

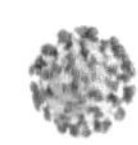
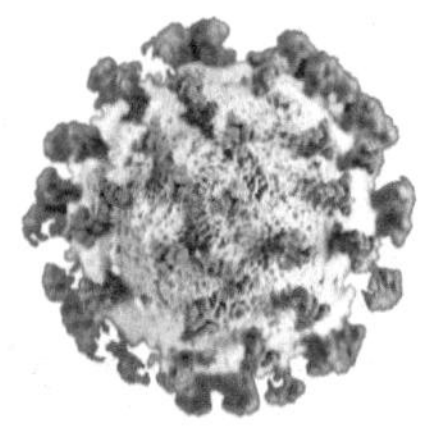
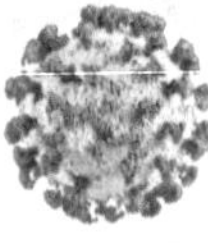
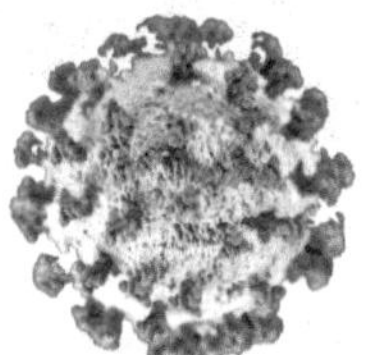
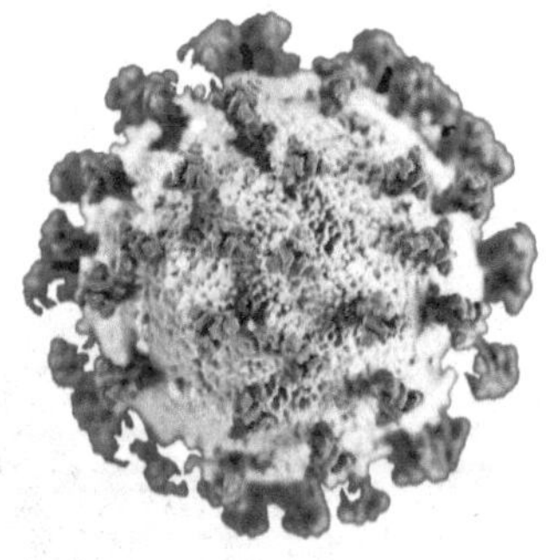

CONTENTS

PREFACE

This is not a traditional diary, so if you are rigid about seeing things as daily entries, you are hereby warned. I refuse to be bound by the diary convention of entering precise dates and times when things occurred. Part of a difficulty of living through the Corona virus time was that so much happened fast and so early on, that it was difficult to keep things straight, much less record meticulously every detail. Nor was it easy to discern what was truly important at the time it happened.

This diary has topical chapter headings to better focus on important epidemic issues, with some monthly timeframe entries, which are often updated later. It covers the period from January 1, 2020 through the end of the year. For Las Vegas and Nevada the Corona Year began on March 1st. Using the topical chapter headings, those interested mostly in specific topics, can go directly there.

The diary format enables one to set up a loose but useful chronology of events. Anyone who lived through this year, somewhere in America, will be able to say that lots of it is familiar. Yet the USA is so diverse that many people will remember Corona as a joke while others will remember mind-numbing terror. Hopefully, some will be fascinated by this narrative of what it was like in Las Vegas, America's glitz capital, a small desert and multi-city metropolitan area of only two million people in a state whose total population is only 3.1 million, not counting roadrunners, coyotes, and rattlesnakes.

My interests as a psychiatrist are to see if a better understanding of this epidemic can be obtained by quiet and careful deliberation. I am not interested in finger-pointing and playing the blame game. There are hordes of people waiting to do that, and most are not even waiting. I hope this narrative will be useful to people wanting to relive and revisit some of the events and find some sort of emotional closure, or if not, at least entertainment.

Sigurd Bergman, M.D.
December 31, 2020
Las Vegas, Nevada, USA

1

THE NOT SO OBVIOUS SECRET
OF THE CORONA POSITIVE NUMBERS
(END OF MARCH)

When I started noting the Covid-19 numbers in mid-March there was something strange about them which I at first could not comprehend. Testing was slow to begin in Las Vegas (insufficient tests available) so tests were only given to people who had initially been confirmed by medical staff to have Covid-19 symptoms. The positive rate (for those tested) was given first as 6.5%. That number did not make sense. It was way too low! Even assuming some people may have had the regular flu or an infection. Slowly the rate climbed to 8% then 10%, then 12%+. No one has ever questioned the accuracy of these lab tests; the target virus was either present or it wasn't.

How could this be? Only one out of eight people at the middle of May, when symptoms were still necessary before you could be tested, had the disease (as confirmed by the lab findings)! Yet seven out of eight people had symptoms of the disease (or said/believed they had symptoms). What we were primarily measuring besides the low clinical incidence of Corona was the incidence of hysteria, histrionicity, and hypochondria. What was measured here was an unrecognized societal panic and mental health problem encased within a public health epidemic.

Hysterics are people suffering from irrational fears. They can't be reasoned with ordinarily because their fear drives out rational thinking. They are seldom amenable to psychiatric treatment and virtually never seek it. Histrionics are sort of high-strung people whose manner of speaking and acting is often theatrical and overly dramatic. People like this might, for instance, have labile (highly unstable) blood pressure. Their blood pressure can go way up beyond its normal level if they are feeling upset. As an example, such a person could present themselves at an urgent care clinic because they have become convinced that they have Covid-19. Given a

Corona test showing negative the emergency doctor would want to retain that person for treatment or refer to a hospital emergency room simply because the high blood pressure level was an immediate health risk more serious than Corona. Had that person gone to a local emergency room in Nevada in a two-week period (end of April) when they were swamped with Covid-19 patients, they might have had to wait for hours to be seen. What do people do then? Some people get angry after waiting nine hours to be seen and walk out. For our labile histrionic patient that was what she did and it was the right thing! Her anger and disgust with waiting drove down her blood pressure to its usual level. What goes up must come down. Hopefully.

Hypochondriacs are people that imagine they have every disease known to man and some that are extraterrestrial in origin. I suspect they are having a field day with Covid-19.

Imagine the possibilities of having a disease that can present with no symptoms! How can you have the disease of Covid-19 even though lab tests say you do not have it? I am sure some such cogitations have been developed by hypochondriacs. I also suspect that hypochondriacs are getting tested twice and more. If they keep hanging around medical clinics long enough, they just might get their wish.

On June 12, 2020, the local newspaper said Las Vegas's positive rate was 5.4%, but when they factored out those people who had been tested more than once, the rate was 4.7%. I feel that's possible proof of the presence of hypochondriacs or hysterics.

Of the three groups just discussed, hypochondriacs are the only ones who love doctors. Why? Because meeting another doctor means finding out about possible new diseases they would like to have. Like a birder collects a life list of birds.

Now back to the mystery of numbers. National numbers (for positive rates) were a bit higher back in April, than Nevada's numbers. But not too much; the rate for women was 15% and for men was 21%. Men were chided by the CDC for "not taking better care of themselves." A remark that sounds sexist to me, and an inaccurate behavioral inference, Doctor! The total for both sexes was 19%. By mid-June that percent had dropped to about 10%.

It was natural for local newspapers to focus on state issues, but the lack of national data on positive rates was a serious reporting oversight. I only saw this number given once in our local paper over many months. They reported the national death rate daily and of course that was responsible reporting. Researchers and statisticians all know that it's important to acquire the largest pool of data when you are studying something, because this gives you more authority to derive scientific conclusions.

In May, Nevada acquired lots of testing kits and testing was thrown open to everyone, whether they had symptoms or not. Thousands were tested and the result for this huge batch was a positive rate of 1½%! Less than two people out of a hundred had the virus! Hysteria was no doubt still operating but probably curiosity was also. The belief they could be symptom-free and still test positive might have encouraged many people to get tested. This muddied the water even more.

At the end of May, Wuhan, China retested all 9 million residents and found just 300 positive cases. That suggests to me that this virus, like the Spanish Flu, will likely be around for two or three more years regardless of a vaccine. It is persistent, sneaky and bounces back in waves. This further suggests to me that national shutdowns might have been a tragic mistake that served no useful purpose and should never again be repeated. Efforts to prevent or limit infection should exist at school, at work, or wherever people gather. Hiding at home is an individualistic solution and not a societal one; little better than sticking your head in the sand.

On June 12th, the positive rate in Vegas was down to 4.7%, almost two weeks after Governor Sisolak's phase two reopening (including casinos, etc.). Then, predictably (because of the usual three week time lag) it went up again as many people "changed position on life's chessboard."

These up and down waves will likely be our future for the next two years or more. They are reason for concern, not overwhelming fear, or reasons for total closedowns. With or without a vaccine we may have to hold the line until we have reached "herd immunity" (when 60% or more of the population has had the virus).

Perhaps one of the reasons people are so scared of the waves is their perception that epidemics should follow neat straight curves (up then down), instead of the raggedy waves we are seeing. These erratic waves just might be visible because that is the natural rhythm of the disease or because we are intervening to try and change the curve. Remdesivir, plasma, and steroids were in use by May and then months later in September, as reported by Dr. Fauci, monoclonal antibodies that stop the Coronavirus from spreading in the body, antibody based medications, other blood products from recovered patients, antivirals, and the anti-inflammatory drug dexamethasone.

On June 27th in Vegas just such an erratic/sudden surge or wave got headlines, but the small print was that it was in younger people (18 to 24 years old) who were not hospitalized and did not die. No one wanted to pin blame on the local Black Lives Matter (BLM) demonstrators but the timeline and age convergence are suggestive.

A slaughterhouse in Germany or an outbreak in Peking are typical of the "localized hot spots" which characterized the spread of Covid-19 during this period. By August, the scale of these outbreaks here and there looked to some people (myself included) as the dreaded "second wave."

Anyone looking at newspaper graphs of U.S. deaths (based on Hopkins numbers) on September 23, 2020 could see proof the dreaded "second wave" was here. The first wave peaked in early April and bottomed out mid-June. The second wave peaked early August and then dipped downward. I heard no discussion of the arrival of the second wave until October though it had been long visible. Nor discussion of its possible significance. Nor have I heard any discussion of how it's possible for national positive rates to be so incredibly low.

On November 6, Nevada saw 1,562 new cases, its highest spike to that date; with 21 more deaths. This looked to me to be Nevada's Third Wave!

CDC experts and later the White House task force all looked at those above-discussed early national positivity numbers and did not see the obvious. They are way too low and mask some secret. The secret is that a positivity rate of 10% (much feared by August) means simply that one out of ten people tested have Covid-19 and nine out of ten people are probably suffering mild to moderate hysteria because they believe they have Covid-19.

This epidemic is also a mental health problem in itself! These numbers are frightening to psychiatrists, psychologists, social workers, and counselors.

This reminds me of Hans Christian Anderson's fairy tale of the "Emperor's New Clothes" where all his subjects raved over the Emperor's new clothes (he was naked).

Of course, one could argue that all the multitudinous medical labs that did the testing are all incompetent to identify a particular virus and EVERYONE tested has the virus and tens of millions more that didn't get tested. Or that all the labs are delivering mostly false negatives thereby making the testing useless and suggesting major lab science incompetence. Unlikely!

From an analytic point of view it seems ridiculous to use the positive test rate as a major measure to control the reopening of the economy, as Nevada did, and perhaps the Feds as well. However, indirect measures (like this) can sometimes work despite logic. In this case, surges in the number of Corona-sick people (seeking medical care) usually correlates with a higher positive rate.

But wait! Life has some further surprises for us. By early September in Nevada the number of new cases plunged with a drop in hospitalizations. All indicators (except the death rate) showed a drop while the positivity rate continued upward (towards 12%). This should have told us that using the positivity rate as a significant indicator was no longer safe. The persistence of a significant death rate is puzzling as well. Could it be a lengthy time lag from the first wave, or is it that there is a tiny number of people who are fatally susceptible to Corona, and the virus is seeking them out? Finding what these people have in common might be one way to lower the death rate.

The real logical meaning of a rise in the positivity rate means fewer people are hyped by hysteria and slightly more are really sick with the bug!

Now you know the closest guarded secret of this epidemic, of which neither the president nor Dr. Fauci were aware!

So, what is the significance of all this? Simply this: the encouragement by medical and governmental entities—influenced by the hysteria of patients—that everybody should get tested whether they felt sick or not, slowed down the treatment of the tiny percentage of this horde that really had the disease. Not recognizing and addressing the hysteria of potential patients who were swamping the system, enabled the real Covid-19 epidemic to surge forward. In short, we shot our own foot. It is not science we did not listen to, it is common sense.

Aspects of this key issue will be discussed elsewhere in the narrative.

2

PRIOR HISTORICAL EPIDEMICS

Of course there have been diaries written about epidemics before but the only one I can recall at this moment is Danial Defoe's "Journal of the Plague Year." "Masque of the Red Death" a short-story by Edgar Allan Poe was a spooky story about people locked together in a house as a plague raged outside.

I mention Poe's story because one of my regular patients mentioned to me over the phone that in the early Corona period when the worst case scenario predictions (computer models) were spinning outward daily from the media like multiple Cassandras, she (my patient) felt like she was waiting for the Red Death to knock on her door. Because of social distancing there was no one to party with nor give her a hug or even hold her hand.

Historical descriptions of epidemics I've always found fascinating, starting with the famous Plague of Athens in 480 BC; they didn't have a clue. When people in fashionable houses all died, strangers walked in and took possession. Life was fast and dangerous. Sickness was a punishment of the gods! Typhus is the suspected culprit.

Barbara W. Tuchman's classic "A Distant Mirror: The Calamitous 14th Century" describes the Black Death (Bubonic Plague) as it raged through Europe and Asia killing millions of people and nearly destroying human civilization and not a soul knew how people got the disease! Nor how to medicate it. Doctors back then were worse than useless; they believed the stars ruled human health and destiny. If you ran away from doctors in those days your chances for survival increased. The only "cure" was running away to the country and hoping no one there was sick and you did not bring the bacillus with you!

No one knew the plague had two non-human vectors (and reservoirs), the rat and the flea. The bite of either meant death. In its pneumonic phase the plague could be passed through the air (like Corona), except after 14 days you were not out of quarantine but dead. Only one researcher in those days (an Italian) came close to part of the truth with his theory of bad air (caused by cosmic influence).

Medical science had begun to make a vast difference by 1917 when the great influenza pandemic called "Spanish Flu" struck. The pandemic continued into 1918 and then into 1919. They say millions died throughout the world and one third of the world's population had it. The number of dead was approximately 30-50 million in a world population of less than two billion people (we have nearly eight billion people now). You can see from these numbers the Spanish Flu was far more deadly than Corona. The flu killed 675,000 Americans which in today's numbers would be roughly 2.7 million dead Americans.

People in America (and most everywhere) were not as healthy as they are today. There were no vaccines and World War I was going on at the time.

Did Spain or Hispanics bring America this flu? Did not happen. Spain was one of the few European nations not engaged in fighting each other and there was no press censorship there so as news of people dying of influenza in Spain got into the press, the rest of the world thought the flu had originated there. In fact, it was decimating the ranks of soldiers on both sides in World War I (and in many countries) but strict press censorship was imposed to prevent war morale from sagging.

How did our forefathers handle things? They implemented quarantines, curfews, stay at home orders, and closing of public places where crowds could gather to avoid spreading the flu to others. Within a month or two all these restrictions ceased and the world went on its way. People worked or went to school and stopped doing these things only if they got really sick.

By mid-May of 2020 it was clear that collecting solid scientific data for a pandemic (simply an epidemic that hits many countries or places at the same time) was like a farmer collecting oranges, apples, peaches, and grapes in one basket. Some countries did not have the medical infrastructure to do it; others had political reasons for looking better than they were. Lying is a human game not confined to politicians and bureaucrats. Bad numbers are little better than lies. Whether the numbers are good or bad, Johns Hopkins collects them all.

On July 11, 2020, the World Health Organization (WHO) announced plans to investigate the origins of this Corona virus in China. It is believed that it jumped from animal sources to humans. Candidates are snakes, bats, and pangolins. It is also believed that the exotic foods, pets, and skin markets (legal and illegal) are to blame.

3

WHO AM I?

I feel a responsibility to tell you who I am before I delve too deeply into the doings of that fateful and crazy year. Especially as I believe most people think shrinks are all bearded Freudians or idiots. I was born forty-six years ago and am a US citizen. I have never had a beard.

I am also a citizen of Sweden. In short, I am a dual citizenship person; that strange animal created by law and politics. My mother and father were vacationing in Las Vegas and my mother got too excitable and I came early. My father, who was a diplomat, thought it would be okay that I should be born in Vegas (in this regard my mother's wishes were paramount and so I came early and that was that). My father and mother thus arranged that I should be a child of two countries and have the extra advantages that brought. To this date I am not so sure that was a good thing for me, but life is full of uncertainties. We must venture forth with what we have been given, and not cry over what we don't have.

My parents should really have called me Janus instead of Sigurd (remember Janus was that Greek two-face) but alas my esteemed grandfather was named Sigurd and that sealed my fate. My wife and 10-year-old son used to call me "Siggie," until they were killed by a drunk driver three months before the Corona year began.

Why did I go into psychiatry? I realized early in my medical career that I had a talent for understanding people, for reading both their body language and understanding their motivations through what they said or did not say. This is a talent I have noticed I shared with some Gypsy fortunetellers and poker players. I went where my talents and interests lay and embarked on a career as a private psychotherapist. Not a Freudian if you please! Swedes are not hung up on sex as are Americans.

I had an excellent marriage for eighteen years. My wife had been a specialty children's surgeon; she was a beacon of warmth and love to all she met.

At the time of Corona's emergence I was at the beginning of a grieving period for my dead wife and child. A bachelor once again, and mostly unemployed like half of Nevada.

Forgive me if I did not mention earlier, if you are reading this to hear lurid details of how I cared for dying Corona patients as they struggled for last breath, you came to the wrong book. I am the wrong kind of doc for that. That is not to say I didn't do something for my sick neighbors in Vegas.

What we were fighting was more than a virus, it was hysterical, unreasoning fear. Because of my wife's contacts in the medical system, I was able to work with other health professionals, including doctors and nurses on intensive care wards, talking to people (necessarily by phone) whose psychiatric response far outstripped their physical ailments. In short, I treated hysterics and histrionics. Sometimes successfully (they lived) and sometimes unsuccessfully (they died). Not until the end did I get any remuneration at all for these activities, and never any acclaim or gratitude.

Of course, I checked in on my regular patients at least once a month to make sure they were weathering the Corona psychic storm.

As I said earlier, I went into psychiatry because I liked working directly with people on an intellectual and emotional person-to-person basis, though my first interest had been epidemiology. Thus, as the Corona craziness began to emerge in mid-March in Vegas, I thought a diary might be worthwhile, if not to others, at least to keep my own head on straight. I could get some experience as a medical sleuth, not directly perhaps, but secondhand so to speak.

Corona seemed like the perfect middle-class disease, 'c'ette nouveau', never been seen before. Clearly more dangerous than your average flu and lots more communicable, but not as serious as the Spanish Flu had been and certainly not in the major league of diseases.

Surprisingly, our leaders, both medical and political, suddenly treated it as imminent disaster requiring societal shutdown. I was puzzled. Perhaps they knew a lot more they were not telling us. That was my first impression, but more about this later.

In June, my wife Aurora and son Zack and I used to hike and camp in various areas within 100 miles of town. Zack was getting interested in the outdoors and dreamed about becoming a Boy Scout. A drunk driver ended that dream. A sick legal system that does not protect society's innocents but bends over backwards to protect the perpetrator was at fault. He had, while blind drunk, crashed two other cars but no one had died in those crashes. I go to all his hearings, not for revenge but for justice.

My situation parallels part of the Black Lives Matter conundrum. How do you deal with the same legal system and unions that protect heavy-handed recidivist cops?

I know burning down a store or sending out a social worker with a bataka (a foam bat used in psychotherapy) to pretend to act as a policeman is unfair and unethical.

I like social workers and have always worked well with them. We have a complex society that requires many different skills. Cops are a necessary part of society. We should cherish and train the good ones and find new career choices for the bad ones. Or maybe find them prison cells. As for social workers, I am sure many of them are on the front lines since they are an integral part of the medical system, a fact little known to our media people.

As of June of this Corona year my hikes have been few but I know where there are lots of red rock tinajas, hidden trails, spectacular petroglyphs, and rare Bear Paw Poppies. The problem is parks keep opening and closing, making it difficult for the public to know what is open. Red Rock State Park and the Thirteen Mile Drive are the local favorite. Social distancing is easy in a car on the 13-mile scenic drive.

Valley of Fire State Park (outside of town) has spectacular hiking, drives and even campsites. Lake Mead is the other favorite for beach, boating and fishing.

Governors have not encouraged their populations to take easy-distancing outdoor vacations, and they should have. Outdoor getaways in a time of indoor curfews are necessary for public mental health. Imagine trying to keep Californians off their beaches. Are these guys compulsive Puritans?

In the late afternoon on June 28th, I saw from town a massive fire breakout on a ridge near Mt. Charleston. The smoke mixed with a cumulus cloud and made the cloud brown! As of July 2nd, the Mahogany Fire was still only 30% contained. A hot spot of the fire was Fletcher Canyon which used to be the location of the scenic and easy Fletcher Canyon Trail. Aurora and I hiked there frequently with Zack. An illegal campfire started by an inept camper started this conflagration.

Mt. Charleston is Vegas's alpine community at 9,000-plus feet elevation. The area has a tiny ski run as well as hiking trails and camping areas. Aurora and I often climbed Mt. Charleston (11,000-plus feet) before Zack was born.

One July a few years before Zack came to share our life, Aurora and I drove a long way to a campground high in the mountains of California. Most campgrounds have little bulletin boards at the entrance which I always compulsively check out. This campground sign warned "Plague Carrying Rodents Have Been Identified in This Campground." Our immediate desire was to turn around instantly but our bladders would not allow us to. We used separate bathrooms to speed our departure.

We had camped at this place before, so we knew we had to leave. No sane person wants to hang around where Pasteurella Pestis has been found! Greenhorn campers fed the ground squirrels, thus they were overtly bold and constantly begged or stole food. These were the likely plague carriers (other places it was chipmunks or mice). Tent campers like us were most at risk.

I was unhappy to read in early July about a case of plague in Outer Mongolia. The article mentioned that the mortality for untreated plague infection was ninety percent. I do not know the back story on that number, but it seems too optimistic. There are antibiotics today that can save plague victims if they get them in time.

Even as a doctor my major source of information on Corona comes from the local newspaper. No one is writing learned papers for the New England Journal of Medicine. What the front line people are saying, when it is reported, is scattered, unorganized, anecdotal, and sometimes contradictory. Only the misinformed think science or medicine always speaks with one voice. As an example, one of the issues that was vital at the end of March, the presence of symptom-free super-spreaders, was still being debated in the middle of June and still into early September and was no closer to resolution.

Las Vegas has only one newspaper, the Review-Journal, basically a hydra with two political viewpoints. In an unusual legal arrangement (reminiscent of my dual citizenship) there is one daily section labeled the Desert Sun, which is independently owned and operated. The Review-Journal is moderately Republican, while the Sun is intensely left-leaning Democratic.

I am not much interested in politics and politicians but am often amused by their antics and utterings. Their behavior is so predictable because of their rigid thinking. Serious compromise discussion no longer has a place in politics. This lack also affects interpersonal relations as well. Even before Corona, I was getting lots of people with very scary personality disorders. Even the legal system was trying to saddle us with impossible patients. How in the world did judges come to believe that psychiatrists could "cure" psychopaths? Anyone who says so is seriously misinformed.

Las Vegas is a nice, almost always sunny, place to live if you like the heat and don't mind the breezes too much (they keep the air clean as well as cool you down). I live in a quiet middle-class neighborhood. I have done well here despite my Swedish genes. Maybe Sweden was much warmer two thousand years ago. Who knows? You need a climate expert/anthropologist for that question. Medical science itself has become very specialized as of late. Not always is this a good development. Our complex world needs generalists also.

I have no maid, no servants, no family here but have recently acquired a boarder by "inheritance." She has deep blue eyes and struts with a sinuous twist of her lovely body. Not a Houri! But a lovely seal-point Siamese named "Ming-Yow."

How did I become associated with this lovely young thing in a city where puppies or kittens are not for sale and all animals are rescues?

In January of this year I was visited by an attorney for one of my deceased patients. My former patient had made me the provisional papa (no one owns a cat) of Ming-Yow, with a three-day exploratory trial visit. If one of us was not happy with the arrangement, Ming-Yow would have to bunk with the patient's niece who inherited three-million dollars. Ming and I became instant chums. That kind of response from any cat is rare. But Ming even drapes herself around my neck like a fur coat that ladies used to wear in the early twentieth century. Some Siamese are that loving and Ming-Yow is that way day and night. She loves my company and the feeling is mutual. If I am a little sad, she licks my hand like a pet dog.

Luckily, there was no hoarding of cat food at local stores. However, as a bachelor re-learning cooking skills I was appalled to find our local stores (late March) without toilet paper, paper towels, Kleenex, hand wipes, hand sanitizer, and sanitary wipes (for cleaning household items). Even bread was hard to come by. There was lots of Spam and canned soup for sale but every time I went shopping something on my list could not be found. What in the dickens were people hoarding olive oil for? For that matter, why were they buying up toilet paper?

Diarrhea was not an identified symptom until late May, and even then, it was rare. People react differently to viral illnesses. Massive amounts of bottled water were also for sale. It is strange because we have a big dam "next door" to Vegas and a very modern and dependable water system. Why hoard water?

One of my neighbors has gastrointestinal difficulties and uses an over-the-counter (OTC) medication called Famotidine, suggested by a gastro specialist. In May, an article appeared in the paper saying this medication (along with dozens of others) was being tested for use against Covid-19. The day after the article came out, supplies of Famotidine were gone from drug store shelves. People were hoarding an unproven medication! Luckily, their memories were short, as July began supplies returned to normal.

By July, toilet paper, Kleenex, and paper towels were back in stores, but never have I seen any "pop-up" hand wipes or sanitary wipes. I think these are permanently gone. Perhaps they are being sold to hospitals or nursing homes and such.

The fact of hoarding itself was a clear indicator of hysterical thinking. Food workers everywhere were dubbed "essential" and there was no reason to expect an interruption of the food supply chain. This irrational hysterical behavior I call "The Venezuela Effect." In the year before Corona, Americans read horror stories in the media about the crashing socialist economy of Venezuela, including shortages of toilet paper, water, food, clothes, etc.

Poor Bernie Sanders. Clearly Corona, with the Venezuela Effect hoarding raised specters of debilitated socialism and was a big factor in his defeat in May. An unusual victim of political hysteria. Future victims, I fear, are coming.

On July 12th I became aware of a new hoarding item, US coins. Merchants have insufficient coins to make change. They are urging people to pay for things by "rounding up" (thereby donating the rounding amount to a charity). Six months ago people were tired of too many coins in the purses and piggybanks and actually paid machines to count (and exchange) their small coin for paper.

I am sure any economic historian will tell you this is a bad sign and feeds inflation by putting upward pressure on prices. It is also hysteria. Next time I go to the pharmacy for small items I will take Aurora's coin purse with dollar coin amounts taped to it. Fight this craziness!

I have become a good shopper. Most people wipe down their shopping carts but I prefer to use light cloth gloves to push the cart around.

I will often use a shopping cart that has been sanitized by the Vegas sun. Of course I use my bare hands to put the items in the shopping cart.

Today's temperature was predicted as 114 degrees; in my neighborhood it got to only 109 degrees. Vegas is a valley surrounded by mountains, similar to a bowl, and predicted temperatures are usually for the bowl bottom, which is considered to be downtown Las Vegas. As the streets sweep gradually upward, it gets cooler. Blue Diamond, a tiny place which does not consider itself part of Vegas, is probably the coolest. But closer in, the Del Webb "highlands" in Summerlin are nearly as cool. One of their mottoes up there is "Don't feed the coyotes, keep your cat indoors."

In Nevada, a number of businesses designated as "critical" were allowed to stay open even from the beginning of the shutdown. Car repair shops for example. My mechanic, who I needed to see in early April, was running a tighter ship than most medical offices at the time. The local UPS Store was amazingly busy. Multi-purpose stores that sold food were open.

By the end of June, most of the hoarding had stopped. Except for pop-up hand wipes and sanitary wipes. The hand wipes I can understand but why sanitary wipes? Were people using these and not reading the labels which warned against their use on people? (Attention dermatologists!) Were they using these to wipe down their kitchens and sinks in ritual cleaning trying to prevent Corona spread? Where there had been no vector of infection, that behavior looks hysterical. Preemptive disinfecting is useless.

In early October, I discovered an unusual hoarding problem. Maybe hoarding is the wrong word; maybe it is a consumption issue. Ice cream! A friend, who is an ice cream dilettante, came to visit. The ice cream section of the grocery store was ravished. The only ice cream left were far-out flavors from companies I had never imagined existed. I knew right then who was getting rich in these Corona times! My friend said, upon being served, "Oh my, this is dairy free vegan!" We ate it but it was not as good as the real McCoy.

4

SISOLAK VS. GOODMAN (EARLY MAY)

Steve Sisolak is governor of the state of Nevada; he is also a leading Democrat. Democrats outnumber Republicans by quite a margin in Nevada, everywhere except in rural counties. Carolyn Goodman is the mayor of Las Vegas. Goodman has rotated her involvement in political parties over the years from Republican to Democrat to Non-Partisan.

From the beginning of the Corona pandemic, Goodman pushed for no shutdown at all then later compromised to "eight days or so." All of these positions were nationally considered "correct" by the Center for Disease Control (CDC) and others early on. Then came the radical decision to shutdown the economy and confine citizens to their homes for an indefinite time.

Sisolak rolled with the tide. Goodman was left standing on the pier watching the crowd go out into a highly troubled sea. The media had already started to paint Goodman as out of touch before an interview on national television in which the host was more interested in making Goodman a political casualty than in actually listening and exploring her view. The notion that Goodman raised that Las Vegans might be willing to be guinea pigs and take a chance on reopening Vegas right away to prevent the economy's destruction made her a national laughingstock. However, I would guess at that time that one-third of Las Vegas's population was ready to do just that.

There are lots of residents here that like to gamble for fun as well as lots of residents who just like the city and never gamble at all. However, hospitality and gambling are the mainstays of the economy. When state unemployment rates were unveiled, Las Vegas was in the thirties (higher than the Great Depression) and the highest in the nation.

Of course, some locals started the "Not My Mayor" theme as well as initiating a recall election. By the end of the first week a groundswell of support for the plucky and principled mayor had developed. Locals could sense that Goodman truly cared for them and the burg and was not a puppet for the money people as she was portrayed.

Although local press coverage of that national interview was hardly favorable to Goodman, within a week things started to happen fast in Vegas. I suspect people such as Nathan and Miriam Adelson, Mr. T., and the casino people met with Governor Sisolak.

Shortly thereafter Governor Sisolak started opening up Nevada rather swiftly. Gambling had been slated to open last under Phase 3. A June 4th surprise early opening (under Phase 2) was unveiled for the casinos! All this time a groundswell of public support had developed for Mayor Goodman (with the "Not My Mayor" slogan dying abruptly). Local small businesses (those that were not already defunct) were relieved with the Phase 3 opening.

My neighborhood Chinese restaurant, which was the best in my part of the valley) was already demolished. A "For Lease & Equipment Forfeiture" sign was posted on the door. Their tables and cooking equipment were gone. Even as I walked away from this neighborhood sadness, I nearly bumped into another man who was looking at the same sad signs on the door and swearing out loud. A fellow Chinese food lover!

In fact, much later (late June) the finest Chinese restaurant in town, which is not located in Chinatown nor on the tourist route, but mainly supported by the local Chinese population was offering only take-out. They were not able to deal with the new constraints faced by all restaurants these days.

Some considerable conjecture suggests that Corona spreads best through the air. Perhaps someone can figure out how to hype-up existing ventilation and air-conditioning systems or add a disinfecting component to them that would suck up or neutralize the Corona aerosols. Or perhaps restaurants could use those virus-killing ultraviolet lamps (a new kind of mood lighting). Even the old-fashioned ceiling fan might have the ability to force Corona aerosols downward to the floor away from where people breathe. Offices and schools might benefit from these ideas also.

Restaurants, schools, and offices could also benefit from developing permanent outdoor venues which would extend the facility's safety margin. This would give people the opportunity to spend part of their day in the open air, away from dangerous confined airspaces. Las Vegas is lucky to have good weather most of the year and may not see rain for months at a time. November 7th brought brief rainfall, our first since spring.

5

THE GEORGE FLOYD KILLING
AND THE CASCADE OF VIOLENCE
(END OF MAY)

My father, the Swedish diplomat, knew Martin Luther King, Jr., both professionally and personally. One of the biggest fears of Dr. King was that the anger and violence of some of his followers, justified or not, would interfere with his people obtaining their political goals.

The Black Lives Matter people are struggling with the same issue, perhaps less successfully. Struggling with something partially out of control, the world turned upside down by the hysteria caused by Corona and a long-term societal lockdown. Some people are a little crazy, others full of violence.

Most of the first demonstrations in Vegas started out peacefully and well-intentioned but as the day (or night) moved onward, the angry people with violence in their heart, who were not content to chant and sing, started to burn, steal, and kill. Hardly a tribute to Brother George's memory.

When the police investigate the crime against George Floyd will they find a racially bigoted policeman? Or just a criminally negligent incompetent, unable to control his own fear and violence. Or both? The difference matters, to both blacks and whites. Sometimes things are worth the wait.

For weeks after Floyd's murder, Las Vegas was the recipient of daily demonstrations by Black Lives Matter people, including college students on long-term sabbaticals. Many of them were from California. Sometimes there were a few dozen, sometimes a few hundred, and once even a thousand. The governor allowed them to break his "rule of 50" in groups even though he continuously denied churches the same right. He did not ask for mask enforcement either.

During this period, demonstrators had an annoying "tactic" of saying to police, "We love you." Reporters did not comment on this, perhaps not understanding its significance or afraid to conjecture. E. E. Cummings, one of the 20th century's most powerful poets, was famous for his "flip-over negations." When he said, "I love you," he clearly meant, "I hate you." Do the demonstrators really believe cops (who did not attend college) were too dumb to know when a mantra of hate is being chanted against them? They know! Hate breeds more hate (like Corona breed more Corona).

At the end of June, BLM demonstrators in Vegas tried a new initiative called "Neutral Observers" which meant law students, special interest lawyers and other "trained observers" wore red and blue shirts to indicate their status. When a group of demonstrators did not move on after repeated requests to do so, the order came from Clark County Sheriff Joe Lombardo to arrest them, shirts and all. Though the mayor complained about the arrests, the sheriff did not back down. The officers said that the neutral observers were in fact not neutral but were acting as leaders of the group.

Compared to other places in America, I think Las Vegans are proud of their police in this harrowing period. They protected demonstrators' right to speech but did not tolerate lawless acts. Maybe when some of the demonstrators from elsewhere go home and talk to others, they might even agree.

When masks became required in Vegas, police refused to arrest people for mask violations (unlike their counterparts in other states) much to the governor's annoyance. Police have indicated publicly that violators will be "educated" on the rationale for mask use.

In July, the demonstrators faced an uncaring, implacable antagonist: the desert sun. On July 12th the forecast was 114 degrees. Demonstrations nearly ceased (much to the relief of hospital emergency room staff). A triple digit heat wave started in July and continued for many weeks through most of August. In August, nighttime lows were often 90 degrees. On August 21 (the day Nevada had a record 38 deaths from Covid-19) the air pollution/visibility was awful from the fires in California. We are downwind from California. And we sometimes create our own heat haze when we are in the summer doldrums (no wind). On Labor Day the city was covered in a grey cloud/fog until mid-afternoon, when an orange sun emerged (a sight familiar to forest fire fighters). The fog never cleared and it was like living in an alternate universe.

A Las Vegas Caucasian mother who had taken her half white/half black daughter to one of the local demonstrations for Floyd, which had been broken up forcefully by the police when violence started, called me that night pleading for me to see her daughter the very next day. Her daughter was expressing extreme fear of ever going back to school and had suffered an "instant personality breakdown" (her mother's words, not mine). The mother's ingenuity in finding me and her quiet persistence and concern for her daughter inspired me to take her case.

Do not say doctors never make home visits. Because of Corona we met the next day in the mother's shaded backyard, in lawn chairs six feet apart and without masks. For two hours in 100 degree heat we had a successful encounter and everyone left happier than when we started. This was in the pre-mask mandated period; it would have been impossible to accomplish anything therapeutic if we had worn masks and all looked like frogs!

During the months of BLM demonstrations, almost all of which violated the "50 max crowd Corona rule" no fines at all were levied on these groups, however, when a private businessman hosted a Trump rally in Henderson on September 13th on his own premises (because other outdoor venues were "unavailable") he was fined the next day. Las Vegas voters will likely remember this act of political favoritism come Sisolak's re-election. The 75+ elderly will remember Sisolak's double-cross on vaccine access. After initially accepting the CDC's intelligent vulnerability analysis, which identified the 75 and older age group as most vulnerable, he tossed them over into "the much larger 70+ pool!"

While looking at television news coverage of one of the summer's BLM demonstrations in Vegas, I spotted a familiar face in the background. He was old but still recognizable. His name is Herbie Cohen and I met him in Chicago 35 years ago when I was a teenager. I went to the location of the demonstration and was in time to find Herbie before he left. When I went up to him and before I introduced myself, he said, "Siggie, you've grown up." What a memory!

Herbie was a legend back in Chicago as a white Jewish survivor of the early bloody civil rights movement days. He helped integrate Rainbow Beach in '61 and made four trips down south. He knew my father and Dr. King. They say Dr. King gave him a letter of introduction which got him in to any Black church in America in his travels down south and elsewhere.

Herbie said he had dropped by the demonstration not to support their efforts but to see what kind of leaders they had now who had so misunderstood Dr. King's teachings. His bitterness over the state of race relations is shown in the extended quote he left with me.

"Institutional racism is a fiction supported by BLM leaders and leftist white intellectual eggheads, whose first big lie is to falsely claim that racism is as alive today and potent as it was fifty years ago. Its second purpose is to lay a colossal guilt trip on people today over their ancestors' actions, in order to extract not equal, but preferential treatment now for Black people.

A parallel convenient fiction that all Republicans are racists first emerged in recent times during Hillary Clinton's 2016 presidential campaign.

Those who preach institutional racism and Republican racism are themselves Black Nazis or Reverse Racists, society's new bigots.

Their hearts and minds are not full of King's or Gandhi's principles, just old-fashioned self-interest and hatred. By their fruits ye shall know them. If you don't know who said that, shame on you! You need more education."

On September 29th, the "Rule of 50" was dropped by the governor for a new general rule of 250 people. Business, particularly on the Strip and in entertainment picked up.

6

THE MANY DISGUISES OF HYSTERIA (JUNE)

Fear is not necessarily bad in all situations; it has survival value for our species (as it does for others). Hysteria is not the same; it is unreasoning and unrealistic fear.

It is normal to be fearful of getting Covid-19 or of dying. These are reasonable fears. There is no certainty you will ever get Corona or if you get it you will even know you have it. However, you can be certain that you will eventually die but all humans know and live with this knowledge. If you take all the recommended precautions you can be happy and get on with your life. If Corona is the total focus of your life you are probably hysterical in your thinking.

There are many specific ways hysteria can be shown. If you have not kept your routine medical and dental appointments for fear of getting Corona at the doctor's office or if you fail to take your children to their appointments or vaccinations for the same reason.

Current media reports on the above two issues tell us that even people with severe medical problems are not keeping their scheduled appointments and doctors are concerned there may be a major die-off from this later.

Speaking of such doctors, I was hoping to have other local Vegas MDs come out publicly linking Corona with hysteria. The guest editorial in the *Las Vegas Review Journal (LVRJ)* by Dr. H. L. Greenberg on August 30, 2020 hit the bulls eye on that. Dr. Greenberg is a board-certified dermatologist. He detailed how fear and hysteria affected two of his patients. A 14-year-old boy had a "severe hand dermatitis because of his Covid-19 anxiety that caused him to obsessively wash his hands." Another patient "neglected her melanoma over a perceived Covid-19 threat...now she has an invasive melanoma."

If you do not answer the telephone because you know your employer is calling you back to work, you are acting hysterically. If you refuse to go back to work knowing you will lose your unemployment benefits, you are acting hysterically and are about to screw up your life. If you listen to politicians who tell you they will take care of you, ask yourself for how long.

If you check the Vaccine Adverse Events Reporting System (VAERS) daily; accept info from self-appointed online medical gurus; or think the vaccine is more deadly than Covid, you are hysterical.

If you take multiple Corona tests, then hysteria, not Corona is your problem. If you think we should give up paper money and coins for Corona you are hysterical.

If you suffer from severe insomina you may be hysterical.

An increase in DUI and serious accidents while driving may also mask individual hysteria behind the wheel.

Early in the crisis I saw several violent non-sensical arguments in an otherwise quiet grocery store parking lot. People nearly fist-fighting over nothing.

A major increase in partisan political bickering may also be a manifestation of hysteria, as may continual fault finding and finger pointing on all sides.

Under ordinary circumstances people do bizarre irrational things like throw razor blades and condoms down toilets. Under Corona that behavior increased as paper towels, non-degradable wipes and other oddities were added. So much so that municipal sewage facilities had to get extra help to manually remove these items before they did serious damage to the systems. Americans, except those who have traveled widely, are ignorant that in some third world countries toilets are not suitable to accept toilet paper, only body waste.

Countries, as well as people, can act hysterically. And many third world countries did in their slavish attempt to imitate the actions and science of the developed nations who locked and shut down their economies.

Most people in the third world suffer from chronic malnutrition in ordinary times. Tens of millions of these were pushed into instant starvation by the economic closures. Some estimate that 30-100 million people will die as a result. This is collateral damage for hysteria and stupidity.

If you are a judge and decide the plaintiffs (Judicial Watch) will prevail and you deny them requested relief, allowing the defendant (the Governor of California) to go ahead with his illegal action of giving cash aid to illegal aliens (which they are not entitled to under California law) then you are acting hysterically, irrationally, and illegally.

In the middle of July, Nevada's governor in responding to a county uptick in cases, shut down all the town's bars again even though 79% of them were in compliance with Corona rules. The local voters (and bar owners) asked, "Why weren't the licenses pulled on the non-compliant ones, and the compliant ones left open to earn their living?" The bureaucrats did not listen. The bar owners sued and lost! The governor even admitted this was probably not the best way things should have been done. Nothing was changed. The bars were still closed. What kind of legal theory suggests it is okay to randomly select certain economic entities to carry without proof heavier economic burden than others for sins (Covid-19 cases) caused by the entire society (county)? It is an old legal theory now resurrected that is called bureaucratic hysteria bean counting.

Another favorite closure target of Governor Sisolak is the state's brothels where legally licensed sex workers (prostitutes if you prefer the old label) earn a living while their unlicensed sisters get all the earnings and probably pass along lively dividends of Corona and venereal disease.

On November 3rd, the *Las Vegas Review Journal* noted that Las Vegas's First Amendment attorney Marc Randazza filed a complaint in Lyon County, Nevada alleging that sex workers using Covid-19 precautions have been unfairly singled out amid the pandemic.

Prostitution is legal in Nevada (by county option) and in a number of small rural counties it props up sagging economies.

At the beginning of this Corona pandemic, travel to this country from foreign lands was shut down out of necessity. Since then states/counties and even Indian reservations have been erecting internal barriers to trade, tourism, and personal travel to visit family or recreational locations by implementing multiple state quarantines and travel restrictions. This is stupidity insular. We are all Americans and those rules are not going to help us rebuild our country's economy. These rules make a mockery of our Constitution.

The president, through the Interstate Commerce Commission and other legal venues, should force governors to rescind their self-mutilating behavior, through the Supreme Court if necessary. As a possible legal argument, don't these various rules look like or have the same effect as tariffs? The federal government is certainly qualified to act on those. This is hysteria at its worst. Are we one country or fifty?

I have a new candidate for hysterical obsession. How about all the people regularly getting a second, or third Corona test? For many months

Southern Nevada's reporting has factored out from the reported rate, the actual "people" rate, which is lower in each weekly test period because some people get a second test. Reporters have shown no interest in this subject. It might be useful to know if doctors are aware of these "repeats" and if there are clinical reasons for it. Or is it just plain hysteria?

As we reached the middle of October, I noticed two things. Drivers were driving wildly and impulsively, particularly in parking lots. They were jackrabbiting in front of oncoming traffic pretending the laws of physics had been superseded for their benefit. This could have been hysteria born of worrying over Corona and the already full-swing presidential election.

I also noticed the number of "cons" tripled, especially on the phone. Hucksters selling free trips to Orlando or identity theft thieves trying to suck up data by pretending to be your insurance company or telling you about a security breach of your computer. Vegas is surely a training ground for these people. They always do their best business when people are "pre-agitated" as they are now.

Some think the hysteria will peak with the election and drop back to normal. I do not think so. If there is no serious negotiation and compromise, we shall deserve the title that some have already given us as "The Disunited States of America." Corona is not the worst problem facing us.

On November 8th, my long-held premonition flowered into reality as Corona hysteria fueled Trump's defeat. We are a primally atavistic people who, while hiding beneath robes of scientific magic, still believe in biblical scapegoats.

7

TESTING AND TRACING/MASKS/THE DEATH RATE: NEVADA VS. CALIFORNIA (JUNE)

The intensive campaign for national testing of the general population and tracing of Corona spread, at the time in late May when we reached the 100,000 people dead milestone, was an example of medical system hysteria. It was a lack of control issue. The 100,000 target had been a hoped-for maximum damage number, and when it was exceeded this reminded the medical system it had been unable to "hold the line." When Justice Roberts said Corona should teach us humility, I think he was referring to the medical establishment as well as the government.

Even though almost all of this fateful number already had one foot and one arm in the grave (from age and serious pre-existing medical problems) Corona got full credit. The way the numbers game is played, the straw that breaks the camel's back gets the full credit for the person's death. Unfortunately, this gives the average person a false impression of the virus's lethality.

Testing and tracing are nearly useless on a fast-moving, highly communicable epidemic like Corona. By the time medical workers find Person A has Covid-19 he or she could have already spread that disease to 50 -100 people (known as a superspreader) or none at all if they are a hermit and compulsive about cleanliness. Time lags are built in to this whole system since it is likely no symptoms were felt for 48 hours after exposure and the person was indecisive for 24 more hours before seeking treatment (time lapse again) and more hours getting tested (time lapse again). If this were a horse race, the virus would be one lap ahead of us at the starting bell. If this were a cartoon, the corona virus would be the

Roadrunner and we the Coyote. If this were a dog, we would be chasing our own tail.

On November 13th, Washoe County Health Officer Kevin Dick, commenting on the latest surge, contributed a new and useful metaphor on the tracing issue (as headlined in the *LVRJ*), "We basically have a Covid-19 wildfire that's occurring...and the idea of contact tracing, where we are going after individual trees that are on fire, is not an effective strategy in that situation."

Because of the above reasons, testing and tracing are mostly attempts to believe we are in control when we are not. They do not affect the onward trajectory of the illness but merely record its path (where it has been) and seldom are they of predictive use. By the time someone has been "traced" by a medical worker, the patient would have noted long before their own symptoms of the disease unless they are one of the "no symptoms" people.

In the middle of August, the debate over the existence of symptom-less corona "spreaders" and their incidence was no closer to closure than it was in the beginning.

CDC says 35% of the people with corona have no symptoms at all. While WHO says the existence of these people is very rare.

On this issue I side with WHO because the notion of 35% of positives being symptom-free is a preposterous notion. No one has ever suggested the possible existence of symptom-less flu sufferers!

In a number of quickie studies and anecdotes, people have been symptom-free for two days after their first contact with the virus and have assumedly infected other people during that time period. That sounds like it is a typical developmental stage of the illness and certainly does not prove the existence of a coterie of symptom-free people walking around unknowingly infecting others.

The WHO position is also convincing because it is known that for other diseases there are "carriers" (like Typhoid Mary, a real historical person), who infected other people with typhoid but did not get sick herself. Thankfully, carriers are also very rare. It is conceivable there are corona carriers. If so, they are likely few and not the cause of any surge because this virus is spectacularly communicable on its own. I recommend introduction of the term "catchy as Corona."

Another reason I do not believe in this symptom-free business is that "denial" is very strong in patients under stress. This means they willfully want not to believe in any evidence they are sick. Willfully closing their eyes because they do not want to believe something. Also, people with mild symptoms may just wish to lie about it so they do not become victims of pariah labeling.

There are personal, ethical reasons the general population may not want to be randomly tested to satisfy the whims of medical researchers. There is considerable stigma attached to getting Covid-19 as some unfortunate patients found out when they got it early and went around telling people they had recovered in a sincere effort to show people it was possible to get the bug and recover. To a lot of people, those who get the disease are pariahs until they also get it.

The unreliability of patient reporting or non-reporting the symptoms of an illness can be clarified by reference to, of all things, vaccines. Vaccines are tested of course, with some patients receiving the vaccine and some receiving a harmless, but ineffective, placebo (often a saltwater solution). What newspaper reporters did not mention until October 30th is that reputable studies are done on a "double-blind" basis. Double-blind means neither the doctor nor the patient know who is getting the vaccine and who gets the placebo. Why is this necessary? For one thing, some patients can "read" a doctor's facial expressions or what is said to them. That is unacceptable because that could affect the outcome of the treatment. The point is that human patients are highly influenceable.

I raise this issue of double-blind in order to shed some needed light on the controversy around superspreaders. In October, Harvard Med was equating superspreaders and carriers. I believe this is wrong. In my definition superspreaders are merely gregarious people with lots of friends who initially do not know they have Covid-19, and who, when they are cured, do not pass it on.

Carriers of diseases I have already discussed. These are rare and to my knowledge no one has yet proved the existence of Corona carriers. Though I believe they are likely to exist, this disease is so ordinarily communicable that it does not need carriers. The CDC believes that 35% of Covid-19 positives are "silent" superspreaders with absolutely no symptoms of the disease at all. These people knowingly or unknowingly continue to spread the disease everywhere, even if they have been identified medically as positive. I believe this is an "urban myth" and unnecessarily spreads further hysteria.

Of course, tracing is a traditional technique which has been used to deal with other diseases such as syphilis or AIDS but not against the flu.

I believe there is already considerable public resistance to being asked tracing questions such as "Did you see Mr. So and So and what was your relationship?" etc. as this next phase is being reached. The tracers may get bored or frustrated from meeting unexpected resistance. Patient resistance to vaccines is likely to show up later also.

Of course, sometimes researchers and tracers get lucky and there is an obvious source of infection and clear cut vectors of infection. The Chinese study of the lady who infected her family (and some nearby strangers at a restaurant) is a de-facto classic. It also showed how the patient's infection droplets were pushed along by the ventilation system. Much useful knowledge came from that but such breakthrough insights are rare.

Also, there is the practical difficulty of measuring significant Corona "encounters." Even experienced tracers are having difficulty with this. From newspaper reports some politicians seem to think being in the Coliseum with a "known Corona positive" (KCP) at the other end is such an encounter. A venereal disease investigator has no difficulty knowing what a significant encounter is.

It is more complex with Corona. How close were you to the KCP? Did you shake hands? Did you touch things they touched? Did they cough or burp in your face? Did they talk to you face to face? Give you a lecture? Slap your face for getting fresh? Were you within six feet of someone for ten minutes or more who later tested positive?

In August, the CDC said if you came in contact with someone who tested positive but you do not have symptoms, do not get tested. Hysterics labeled this as gross negligence, not understanding that the flood of negative test results were drowning out or slowing down the discovery of the positives. One must live in the real world, not an imaginary one. There is no quick, simple, accurate and inexpensive Corona test at this time.

There are "quick tests" which give results in fifteen minutes but they trade speed for accuracy. This issue is discussed elsewhere in more detail.

Two specific quick tests, Quidel Sofia and BD Veritor were banned in Nevada on October 2nd by state medical staff. Used in nursing homes these tests identified currently existing Covid-19 in patients but were poor at identifying people who do not have Covid-19. In other words, they created loads of false positives (identified people has having Covid-19 who did not have it, as confirmed by lab tests).

When Nevada banned their use on October 2nd, the feds told them they were wrong to do so. I side with Nevada. This is an ethical issue that should be left to states to manage. To tell nursing home patients they have COVID-19 when it is likely they do not is wrong. The first part of the Hippocratic Oath is to do no harm! That includes psychic harm.

As Mark Pandori, Nevada's Chief of Testing said in the November 12th *LVRJ*, "If false positive individuals are put into quarantine along with other truly positive people, that is very bad."

By September there was medical concern and a big push to get people to get their flu shots early. Hopefully, this time Nevadans will do better than their usual 39% flu shot uptake rate. Some even fear a stronger than usual appearance of Seasonal Affective Disorder (SAD). This is a specialized kind of depression that usually does not present much in Nevada because we have lots of sunshine year round.

MASKS

On June 26, 2020, Governor Sisolak, in consultation with his medical advisory staff, mandated face coverings for most people in most situations. His advisors, including Brian Labus from UNLV Public Health, have consistently given the governor realistic as well as medically accurate advice.

The mask mandate was long expected and even in the first days, compliance was high. Here is the real problem with masks. We all look like frogs. People (including psychiatrists) can usually "read" other peoples' emotions by looking at their face and masks take away that ability. An even bigger problem is for the police where witnesses are having a more difficult time identifying criminals.

I accept the belief that people, when they are around others especially inside a building, should wear masks. However, I do not believe the scientific position for that view is solid enough to criminalize the non-use of masks.

One of the major arguments for masks is its usefulness against the symptom-less spreader. Since I do not believe in these "ghosts" I am not impressed with this argument. I do believe what medical workers believe, that wearing masks reduces the volume of the virus and thus gives them some protection. People with mild symptoms, or those not wanting to be stigmatized, are going to be spraying out fewer viruses.

However, the major function of masks is to give people a hope or belief they are safe. This may lull people into getting too close to each other and thus put them at higher risk from aerosols. Life is a constant tradeoff.

For the above reasons, my support of masks is shaky.

August brought a new kind of demonstrators to the Vegas streets in the heat of summer; these were locals focused on fighting the mask requirements.

Another important measure in dealing with Covid-19 is antibody testing. This does not measure the incidence of active Covid-19 but it measures people who have likely had it recently. However, some antibody tests, called Quick Tests, are used to identify current COVID-19 by people like politicians and public figures who do not mind trading accuracy for speed. Rapid tests detect certain proteins in the virus.

There is much controversy over what antibody tests are accurate and which are not. This is an area of constant scientific bickering. Some fuss over test selectivity and sensitivity or false positives and negatives.

Despite this fussing, what all the antibody tests cumulatively show is that Corona has been far more widespread than positive tests show now. That means its potency has been way overrated and the death rate very much lower than previously believed.

In late September, a new controversy emerged with the desire by many medical researchers to have antigen positive findings mandatorily included in official state counts of Covid-19 along with the slower, more accurate laboratory Polymerase Chain Reaction (PCR) tests which detect genetic material in the virus and must be laboratory processed.

Those pushing for this viewpoint argue we are otherwise not addressing the full scope of the epidemic. As I write this on September 22, 2020, the first day of autumn, we are a few lives short of our 200,000 dead tally. By tomorrow morning we will have passed it.

On July 1, a new measurement was unveiled in Las Vegas. For every new case of Covid-19 discovered in Las Vegas there would be 1.56 more people who will get the disease. A predictive multiplier that is a traditional epidemic measurement tool but it has not been mentioned until now. It is hardly useful for a highly communicable and erratic virus.

People walking outdoors without masks is perfectly okay if there is very little human traffic around. Attention New Yorkers: there are such places. Use common sense; if someone is coming towards you, move off to give each other room. Or turn your head away at least. If you are a protestor out of doors and you are going to be haranguing or singing at the public it is a sign of medical and personal courtesy to wear a mask.

As for people who wear masks while walking or bicycling outdoors in quiet neighborhoods with few people about or riding alone in their cars, I pity them because they are suffering from PTSD/Corona trauma!

I met such a masked elderly person walking in my neighborhood while I was speaking to a neighbor, who having just passed 60 years of age was in the biggest vulnerable category and having twice survived major cancer surgery was in a newly-discovered vulnerable category. It was 100 degrees and I said to this elderly masked walker that it was not good for his lungs to wear a mask under the circumstances; my neighbor chided him also. His response was, "I know four people who died of Corona."

This was on June 21st and Vegas's death toll stood at 397, so that man knew in excess of 1% of the town's total dead! Of course this is not entirely impossible but I suspect he meant he knew of four people (like the friend of a friend). When people are caught up in fear, they are prone to exaggerate.

If you tell them that the likelihood of their dying from Corona is 1 in 10,000 (about the same as being struck by lightning) they are sure their number will invariably come up. If you tell them these are the same odds as driving your car across town at rush hour or donating a kidney to a relative, they give neither a thought. Those people are suffering from hysteria PTSD/Corona.

The Death Rate: Nevada vs. California

On June 21st, the cumulative adjusted death rate (for 100,000 people) was 415 people for California, and 397 for Nevada. California, which started their lockdown first and was far more stringent than Nevada (who started lockdown toward the middle of the pack) did worse on this key epidemic measurement!

Any claim by California's Governor Newsom that early and strict shutdowns "saved lives" is political hogwash for California voters. It also suggests it is likely folly to extend lockdowns or initiate new ones to deal with second waves.

Of course, over the coming months those numbers might change so it is good to keep cumulating these numbers. The press, to play up the increase in cases in many places in July has resorted to giving results in snapshots of 7 or 8 day rolling averages. That may sell more papers now but it impedes understanding the big picture which can only be glimpsed by cumulating the results to the end of the epidemic. As economists say, "Look to the bottom line!"

8

LAS VEGAS TALL TALES: THE MURDER OF SENATOR FOURFLUSHER, CRUSADE OF THE THREE BROTHERS (JUNE)

In July, Aurora and I used to visit our friends Monica and Carlos Munguia. Monica was a pediatrician and Carlos a literature and writing teacher at UNLV. They turned their pool heater off in the middle of June so the swimming was great.

This July I went alone. When Carlos found out I was doing a diary book, he convinced me that I should include some humorous Las Vegas tales written by two talented writers he has "discovered." All the stories were good and had a connection to Vegas, so I agreed. They might add some color to my narrative as battling SARS-CoV-2 is not an enterprise rife with laughs. I suspected one or more of the stories might be Carlos's but what does it matter? There are three altogether. The first two benefit from brief introductions. The third does not.

The first humorous tall tale was written in the style of Mark Twain and is about a Las Vegas crime from a few years ago that never made a big splash in the national news but made a splash or two in the local media.

THE MYSTERIOUS MULTIPLE MURDER OF EX-NEVADA SENATOR FOURFLUSHER

What was at first believed to be a crank call from an agitated birdwatcher from the Lake Trail area of Las Vegas Floyd Lamb Park last Thursday dawn, turned out to be a bonafide message of sorrow for the political community of Nevada. The mauled, mutilated, and murdered corpse of ex-Nevada Senator Florin Fourflusher was found floating in the primordial swamp ooze at Tule Springs.

The 911 operator, Molly Maguire, first believed the caller was reporting the sighting of a "dowitcher." But this dowitcher was pecking at the hairs (and few he had to spare) on the head of a body face down in the cattail swamp of this historic site about to be transformed into the Tule Springs National Monument. To the chagrin of federal archaeologists, the body was sitting right on top of a 13,000-year-old Paleo-Indian hunting camp.

Local police investigating this gruesome murder were accosted noisily on-site hours later by FBI agents who arrived in force and demanded our local men in blue leave the crime scene to them. Crime scene usurpation it was! A triple claim of jurisdiction was that Senator Fourflusher was one-quarter Paiute-Kickapoo. Tule Springs was essentially a "Federal Reservation" and there was evidence the senator was the victim of an anti-Muslim "hate crime."

A pre-burial memorial was held the next day for Florin at the Church of the Open Mind in Foggy Bottom, while the FBI back in Nevada looked zealously for the murder weapon which was believed to be a thin stiletto sword until an agent tripped over two hot dog skewers and empty hot dog packages in the picnic area.

During his many years in Washington, Florin was remembered for his enthusiasm for the Washington Redskins. He considered himself not a "wonk" but a "pointy-headed egghead." He was an early promoter of "virtual reality."

"Who the hell wants the real thing? Life is messy, just sip the honey."

Florin's fishing pals, like "Luke the Fluke" remembered how he showed them a snapshot of a 500 pound striper he claimed he caught in Lake Mead. "It looked like one of them Ukrainian military photographs, you know, all fuzzy and muzzy. Could have been a fish, could have been a manatee, could have been an ugly mermaid."

Senator Fourflusher's political accomplishments included starting the No More Taxes Ever (NMTE) Movement as well as several contributions to political semantics. For example, he was considered the architect of the "Extreme Terrorism" phrase now so useful to the president. He never, even in his wild youth in rural Georgia, used the "N" word, and was adamant in walking away from erudite scholars, historians, and cooking show hosts. He maintained that a "spade" meant only a suit in a card deck except when it meant that funny tool the braceros used.

He was a man of the people. He never drank that sissy wine (champagne) the Frogs drank nor even that hearty Jack Daniels whiskey so beloved of southern politicians and foreign diplomats. No sir, his favorites were Night Train, Boone's Farm, and that old no-nonsense Thunderbird.

A break in the case came yesterday when an ex-Serbian terrorist, Vlados Vladosky confessed to the FBI that he killed that SOB, "Because the senator let those Muslims get away with it." This confession pleased the FBI because it dovetailed with their preconceived notions of jurisdiction and motive. However, they were discombobulated when another candidate, Esteban Gilhooley, showed up to also confess the murder of Fourflusher.

Esteban claimed that Fourflusher had a steamy "sexual encounter" with his girlfriend Maria Maravillosa, an ascending porn star, last Wednesday evening. Forensic experts found both claimants' fingerprints on the hot dog forks and the bottles and alas, Florin's blood on both forks. Was this a weenie roast gone sour or murder on the night train? Whatever else can be said of him, the senator was certainly a man who died for his beliefs.

A call to Harry Reid's office to discuss the political implications of the Senator's death received a, "No comment."

Senator Heller's office said, "Senator who?"

Governor Sandoval, interviewed in person by this reporter in Carson City smiled and shrugged his shoulders and said, "Quien Sabe?"

The Crusade of the Three Brothers

Introduction

In 2019, left-leaning politicos were accused of incentivizing poor Central American Hispanics to crash the border wall in order to embarrass El Presidente Norteamericano.

As usual, political bigwigs covered their tracks successfully so no zucchinis were served. However, the re-telling of this adventure by one of its participants, Martin Bolivar Juarez, created a sensation throughout Latin America and became an instant folk tale fable. It gave impetus to Brother Martin's writing career. Here is the story just as he wrote it (translated from Spanish).

La Cruzada De Los Tres Hermanos (The Crusade of the Three Brothers)

The Three Brothers combined together in alliance for mutual gain. Their mutual gain was to give el Imperio del Norte a hard time, and they did. Check your phone or computer. This is how it happened.

Juan Pedorro y Puerco was a good for nothing playboy, a tradeless idler but he had a tongue that could charm the birds out of the trees and the girls out of their blouses. This native Costa Rican Hispanic never crossed the Atlantic but surely his mother must have kissed the Blarney Stone while carrying him or perhaps somewhere hidden in the Mayan jungle was a stone idol with the same powers.

Jose Gracioso was an infidel from Spanish Morocco whose religion taught him who and how to hate; he had learned well.

Martin Bolivar Juarez, a native Venezuelan, was a highly educated sophisticate who had more college degrees than coins in his pocket. He had been a child prodigy in several fields.

What turn of fate's wheel brought them together at the disreputable Caracas inn called "El Gallo Cansado" (The Tired Cock)? By the time all the coins in their mutual pockets disappeared, they had drunk many glasses and concocted an alliance that was to make history and scare the US State Department and the Pentagon silly.

As with all great politico/military moves throughout history, it was conceptually simple but a bit hard to execute. They planned to direct tens of thousands of land-hungry and just plain hungry peasants towards the border fence of El Norte in the belief that overwhelming numbers and exuberance would break through, especially the masses who thought that they as gate crashers were fondly welcome to America's perennial party, the land of promise for the hungry, the landless, the harassed, and the unlucky of the whole world. Bravo America!

Most great deeds founder before they are done, for lack of "dinero." Such was our three friends' situation this night. An angel appeared to them in the form of a gringo Americano, nombre de Senor Murillo, who had overheard their discussion and supported their goals on behalf of an American politician, Eduardo Smith of Las Vegas, Nevada. Mr. Murillo promised each of them five hundred American dollars if they would show up sober the next day at noon at an address on the outskirts of Caracas to begin shepherding pilgrims on their way north. He carried out his promise and also promised each of them a thousand dollar cash bonus if they visited him at the Casino De Oro in Las Vegas within ninety days.

Did these paisanos know that America would not welcome these pilgrims when they came knocking at their border fence? Who can say? They believed what they want to believe, as most people do. They had heard so many stories of the welcoming gringos who made santuarios for all. Except no one told them these nice santuario folk would not be waiting at the wall with welcome banners and empanadas.

Los Generales Juan, Jose and Martin were part of the rabble arrested at the last failed charge against the wall. If asked they would have spoken proudly of their failed generalship. Since they had not bathed or shaved for a month, had no sword or braid, and could not speak Spanglish, they were sent south immediately while Pentagon staff looked morosely and ambitiously for Al Queda or Soviet spies. A nice bilingual border guard, Senor Garcia Lorca, told them there was no Casino De Oro in Las Vegas. Ay caramba! Asi termino la Cruzada de los Tres Hermanos. Que lastima!

9

RATIONALE FOR THE
LOCKDOWN/SHUTDOWN/STAY HOME ORDERS
(JULY)

Humpty Dumpty sat on a wall,
Humpty Dumpty had a great fall,
All the king's horses and all the king's men,
Couldn't put AMERICA together again.
—Adapted from a Traditional Nursery Rhyme

It was the last week in March when I first started having doubts that American medical leadership was steering us in the right direction. Most of their directives seemed like pseudo-scientific hunches and anecdotes rather than certain scientific knowledge.

Of course they knew the virus was likely to be similar to its first cousin, the seasonal flu, which kills an average of 61,000 Americans a year (according to the CDC). They knew Corona was more dangerous and three times more communicable. They also knew it was no way as virulent and potent as the Spanish Flu had been. That flu killed 675,000 Americans when the world's population was one-quarter what it is today.

Why didn't they treat Corona as just a super-flu, leaving the government and economy alone, except for immediate rules limiting crowds, pushing social distancing, etc.?

I do not remember media reports I considered inflammatory or exaggerated per se but I know how crowds think and react to constant bad news; many people get hysterical. The multiple competing computer projections from 100,000 to 3 million dead as well as swamped emergency rooms did not help. It seems to me that few Americans were knowledgeable about basic health and biology and thus were easily frightened. Perhaps schools, except for the college bound, are not teaching these basics.

I am a phlegmatic person as I do not excite easily and I take a while to think about things and make up my mind. Some say that is a Swedish trait but others deny it. What does it matter?

What bothered me the most was the shelter in place orders (national lockdown) which many people view as house arrest based on the anti-common sense premise that people who are not sick should be sent home from work and school. Also extreme was the abrupt closing of most public and government facilities, even those where crowds do not gather.

CDC issued early directives suggesting that closing a school was an extreme measure and should be done only for a few days. Ignoring this advice, school districts and governors suddenly went into panic mode and permanently closed schools and businesses nearly everywhere. This spurred further closures and draconian orders.

It is as if our business, political, and medical leaders looked at dramatic media reports coming from China, got spooked and decided, with awfully poor judgment, that what authoritarian China did should be a model for a Western Democracy! They were overreacting to the disease's communicability and were overestimating the virus's potency, as they had done with Swine Flu.

Potency is measured by the death rate, over time. Even then, they saw the death rate in China dropping to a fraction of one percent but for some irrational reason they believed it would not continue to do so. In this kind of epidemic the death rate starts out high. Part of the reason has to do with the mathematics of the counting process. Partly it is because the sickest people succumb first but as it sweeps through the general population most people get only mildly sick so the death rate drops quickly.

At this time, we seemed to be acting like sheep, not thinking people. California and New York seemed to have led the way and the country followed. Early CDC requests for home quarantine orders were for one week. How did a "pause" turn into permanent sequester? Did medical staff truly lead or were they led by political leaders? And what effect did the media horror stories have? It is understandable why New Yorkers reacted aggressively; the virus jumped from China to Europe to New York.

China and Italy's experiences seemed to confirm that old and medically fragile people were the disease's overwhelming targets and children were relatively immune. If so, why send children home from school and workers home from their jobs? These are both irrational responses. The target was always the elderly and sick. Why did our leaders insist on closing down the day to day workings of our society? This did not help the old and medically fragile but it did vastly hurt the young, the strong, and the employed.

Why did they believe that sending everyone home in a national shutdown would enable them to dodge the virus or get it in lesser numbers? Ostensibly it was to keep emergency rooms from being overrun. By moving people from one place to another you do not necessarily make people safer. You just give them a new set of people they can be exposed to or expose in turn. It is possible that sending the children home to a sick parent or family member would cause them to get Covid-19 because of continuous exposure. Whereas, if they had been in school, they would have had much less physical contact and might not have gotten it. Likewise, a sick worker at home all the time is certainly likely to infect their domestic partner sooner. Remember, a person can be sick but have no symptoms or so they say. I have my doubts but that is a complex medical and psychological issue.

I am not arguing that it was worse or better, medically speaking, to confine people at home but that it was impossible to know which alternative was best because we knew and still know very few solid facts about Covid-19. We just cannot know all possible opportunities and routes of infection with a particularly communicable infection like Covid-19.

Covid-19 is like that musical game "Musical Chairs" they play at parties. As the game proceeds everyone keeps going until one person is the winner sitting in the only chair left. In one variant of the game, the last chair is yanked when the music begins again. The people playing are constantly saying to themselves, "If I had only turned right instead of left, I would have been the winner." But they are wrong because the essence of the game is its total pre-planned unpredictability. So it is with Covid-19. Shelter in place orders possibly will make no difference in the death rate in the long run.

The argument for keeping hospitals free for the hypothetical steady increase of patients does not play well with the facts. A sudden surge occurred, which was unpredictable. In New York, and elsewhere, "instant hospitals and ICUs" came into being as citizens across the US helped each other. No corona patient in Nevada lacked for a hospital bed. Of course, those people that ordered shelter in place are bound to continue believing in it.

What was predictable was the drastic effects of shutting down our economy. Hysteria overruled rationality.

I was hoping to find a rational basis for all these extreme actions taken by our medical and political leader. I never did. On April 1st, I reached the conclusion that it was a drastic mistake to shut down the country and shelter in place. This decision was both foolish and cowardly. We should have stood our ground, stayed at work and school, and started learning how to cope with it as Sweden did. And perhaps other countries who do not bang their drum.

In a complex society like ours, everyone has to do their part. Asking some people to take the risk while others hide at home weakens our survival prospects as a unified nation.

Did anyone besides myself consider that Corona might imitate the Spanish Flu and hang around for three years or more? Given that possibility an economic lockdown sounds like societal hara-kiri!

Why did our leaders make the radical decision to shut down? First, they had a strong desire for control as they mistakenly believed the Chinese had exercised. Second, Americans no longer have "problems," everything is a "crisis." That attitude has an undertone of hysteria. Thirdly, some of our political leaders had at least an unconscious shared wish to see a doomsday crisis that would rid them of our current president with whom they are obsessed. Some call this Trump Derangement Syndrome. It is not a conspiracy in the usual sedition sense but it works out to be one. Monsters from the id are extremely powerful as psychologists know. This is a whopper, fueled by hysteria and hate. For those who prefer analogies from history rather than Jungian psychology, consider Thomas More and the King and "Who will rid me of this damned priest?"

Listening to only the most gloomy of public health predictions, our leaders decided that Corona fit their needs, especially as it offered a credible excuse for the destruction of the Trump economy by lockdown and the dramatic but unjustified closing of schools. As Montaigne said, "Men under stress are fools, and fool themselves."

Historian Barbara Tuchman wrote a book entitled, "The March of Folly" in which she argues that governments sometimes pursue paradoxical policies harmful to their own best interests. I nominate the Corona Craziness for study by current historians ambitious enough to follow in Tuchman's footsteps.

"Father Knows Best" is ancient American folklore. When Dr. Fauci admitted Corona was his worst nightmare, the media, along with some of our prominent public figures, elevated Dr. Fauci into a public icon because they despise the president and do not want to look to him as their leader.

"NOT MY PRESIDENT!" They crafted Fauci into their Tin God/Father Figure/Savior. Do not blame the man because it was not his fault. He is a hardworking doctor, scientist, and public servant.

I felt sad for him when his path crossed that of Senator Rand Paul of Kentucky, who is also a doctor, when Paul said, "You don't look like much." Paul is a fearless political gadfly and political animal; he was reacting to Fauci's media image. At another time and place their meeting might have been friendlier.

Paul's and Fauci's relationship was fated to continue being prickly. On September 24th, Paul contended that Fauci and the government team were wrong when they insisted a shutdown was needed to deal with the Covid-19 crisis. Paul might have felt Sweden had been successful without a shutdown so why would the US need one.

Fauci said Paul continued to misunderstand him and said something to the effect that the shutdown was necessary. Fauci's response was less than clear because the full text of their comments was not provided by the media.

10

JULY: THE MONTH OF GOOD OMENS

On a cool (83 degrees) July 4th, at eight-fifteen a.m. I noticed something stirring outside my sunroom window; there was a massing of dragonflies flitting about like daytime bats, eating all the bugs in the air. There is a lake near my house and the flying fish food (harmless midges) periodically fill the air and provide the fish with breakfast, lunch, and dinner. This spectacle can freak out visitors who have never seen midge swarms; they are afraid they will swallow a hundred midges in one breath or open mouthful. Too bad we cannot train midges to gobble up Corona viruses. To a Corona virus a midge would look like Godzilla!

The windchime outside my bedroom is also a dragonfly and it was tinkling and seemed to interest an early hummingbird. A strange morning! By eight-forty-five the dragonflies were gone because the temperature increased to 87 degrees.

I expected swallows, not dragonflies, but they are both beautiful and eat bugs. Routinely, every June, the swallows come to my neighborhood like their appearance at the Mission San Juan Capistrano in California. Their swooping aerobatics are a wonder to behold but they did not come this year. Lots of usual flyway migratory birds and other waterfowl I see in our neighborhood like kestrels, flickers, and grebes did not show up. Attention Audubon Society.

I am not a professional birder though it appears to me the bird migratory patterns have been disrupted, probably due to global warming and weather changes. Nature abhors a vacuum; birds and bugs adapt and the dragonflies took the place of the swallows. Now, if you are a Vegas residential property specialist, I have given you clues to the four possible locations where I live.

Of course, I am much too modern to believe in miracles and omens but I would like to think we are at least over the first high hurdle on this, our country's birthday, in our battle against the SARS-CoV-2 bug, though

I expect Covid-19 to be around for a couple years yet. It is these first frights that are the freakiest!

So, what are these virus bugs like? Not like the bugs in "Starship Troopers." Skipping a biology lecture, it is easier to think of them as being a tiny life form (without DNA) that is a mindless sex fiend, compulsively doing nothing but replicating itself when it finds conditions it likes.

Meaner and more communicable than the regular flu but nowhere near the most dangerous bug around. Not a danger to the human race unless hysteria and stupidity become aligned with it.

Dusk on the 4th was the same as it had always been. Our neighborhood was noisy and colorful from home fireworks both in front and behind my house but they started winding down early. In better times they did not stop popping until midnight.

On July 15th, (the Ides of July) shortly after full dark I saw another omen that was visible in the entire valley, the appearance of Comet NEOWISE.

Visible to the naked eye but when I put binoculars to it, it was spectacular. As bright as Sirius, with a scintillating tail that glittered like a trail of kids' sparklers. What does all this mean? Maybe it was a reminder that despite all the business closures and disruptions, Vegas still had its sparkle. Let's hope.

On July 17th, there was another omen of sorts, or if you wish, a Corona craziness. A mountain lion was spotted near an elementary school in Summerlin (the 4th top rated community in the US). After sedation it got a free ride back into the surrounding cooler mountains. Little did the lion know, there was little likelihood any kids would be at the school for a long time as the school board fussed, fiddled, and feuded.

On July 26th, I saw a rare omen: a twenty-foot-high tube waterspout! I was looking at the lake near my house to see if any wild ducks had flown in recently and suddenly a whippy wind swirled the water into a waterspout. That is the water equivalent of what desert rats call "Dust Devils," little cyclonic winds which are not that rare in the deserts surrounding Las Vegas. What does it mean? Maybe it means we are all mixed up about things (scientists too).

On August 4th, near dawn, out a window of my house, without binoculars, I saw the comet NEOWISE again. Astronomers had said it would be visible this month only with binoculars or telescope. Wrong again. There is a lot of guessing going on.

11

TO GYM OR NOT TO GYM, THAT IS THE QUESTION (JULY)

I am not a weightlifter but Aurora and I used to work out at a small local gym before Covid-19. Our son was not old enough for that activity. When I heard they were reopening, I called to talk about how they were going to run things.

Most of the articles I read on gyms suggested that they were dirty, dangerous places full of germs and a virtual death trap. My personal experience has been otherwise. I used cloth gardening gloves (non-slip) to work out for several years just to keep from getting the ordinary flu, which is easily transmitted by barehanded users. Many people were quite religious about wiping down all the handholds on equipment they had just used.

Some people even wiped down parts of machines that other sweaty parts of their body had touched. I always felt this was simply over-compulsive behavior but apparently there are lots of people who believe you can get the virus from someone else's sweat by pore absorption though the skin. I am no expert but I have never heard or read about such transmission being possible. If it is, you would need to wear a full-body warmup suit which is no fun in Vegas.

The gym planned to reopen by using reserved one-hour slots for people to workout, after which a fifteen minute cleanup by staff would take place. You could reserve back-to-back slots to get a two-hour workout period but you would have to walk the hallways or go outside in the heat for fifteen minutes.

The fifteen minutes of cleanup after every hour of use was hardly that useful, I think, in preventing infection. If they mandated the use of gloves whether latex, cloth or other, they could probably do just as well by doing a half-hour cleanup during the lunch hour and at end of day. In that way their scheduling would not be so chopped up. Some people do fine with only a one-hour workout but I am slow in everything I do. I take a long time to warm up most days and everyone is different.

The major aspect of the plan was to limit the gym to only ten people at a time. In this central regard, I think they were right on because Covid-19 is most of all air and breathing transmittable. In a gym, if you are working hard, you are breathing hard. In a gym the size of mine in the pre-Covid-19 period, thirty to forty people could have occupied the gym so the limitation to ten people is a brave gamble to keep occupancy to twenty-five percent of capacity. Lots of businesses like indoor restaurants are probably not safe at fifty percent occupancy unless bolstered by super cooling innovations with antibacterial and antiviral aerosols. Is anyone working on that?

The above two sentences were written in July. On November 2, 2020 in the *LVRJ*, I got my answer. Bipolar ionization systems that emit positive and negative ions that attach to pathogens in the air and effectively disable them by removing a hydrogen molecule now exist. These systems are being installed in the ducts of Clark County School District (CCSD) nurses' offices (about 850 schools) by the mechanical equipment company Norman S. Wright.

In the end, the unwieldy nature of the gym reopening plan turned me off for now so I use some hand weights at home and I jog to keep fit.

What is important is that people are trying to create a new normal as we will not see the old normal for a very long time.

12

SWEDEN FOUGHT CORONA WITHOUT A SHUTDOWN (JULY)
"QUANTULA SAPIENTIA MUNDUS REGITUR"
("BY HOW LITTLE WISDOM IS THE WORLD GOVERNED")

Swedish Chancellor Oxenstierns' lament over the Peace Conference following World War I

Although I have relatives in Sweden, I am not in regular contact with them, especially during this crazy time as we are all learning to live with Covid-19. My knowledge of what is going on there is limited to my local newspaper which often features upbeat human-interest, international Covid-19 news. There was an article about a 113-year-old Spanish woman (born in the US like me), living in a nursing home in Spain who contracted Covid-19; she got over it and went back to what she was doing before the pandemic just like the 103-year-old Italian lady!

In March or April I remember reading that Sweden's restaurants and bars were open, though people were being advised to social distance. What we were not told was that schools were not closed and there was no lockdown but there were rules against large group gatherings. About that time, Rand Paul praised Sweden's approach and many letters to the editor grumbled about Paul and those idiotic Swedes. In March and April, Sweden's per capita death rate was higher than most Nordic nations.

In May, there was a report that some study in Sweden had identified a thirty percent Corona T-cell count (antibody test).

All antibody testing is controversial. What that little tidbit of information might possibly suggest is that lots of Swedes had gotten the disease earlier than in other places. Whether this is a bad thing or a good thing is not clear. My last chapter will address this issue. Another possibility is they were earlier exposed to a different Corona virus.

On July 17th, according to John Hopkins University, the Covid-19 death rate per 100,000 people was 42 for the US and 55 for Sweden. At this early point it looked like we were doing better than Sweden.

On September 21st, according to *LVRJ* commentator, Jacob Sullum, "The per capita fatality rate in the US recently surpassed Sweden's rate and the gap is growing because the cumulative death toll is rising much faster in the US."

Mr. Sullum believes that despite all the criticism leveled against it, Sweden may be now faring better than the US and "lockdowns may not be the best approach."

On October 7th, an editorial in the *LVRJ* headlined, "Swedish Virus Model Not Looking So Bad Anymore." Some comments were, "The numbers of Swedes dying from COVID-19 has declined steadily since March," and "Sweden is doing far better at containing the virus than many other European countries grappling with renewed outbreaks," and "Sweden serves as an indication that respecting peoples' liberty does not inherently pose a health threat." The editors believe a national lockdown here would be a mistake and I agree with them.

On October 13th, WHO announced that it was not recommending that lockdowns be used as ordinary ways of fighting Covid-19 and should be a last resort and only for a short time for emergency readjustment.

I believe this is an astute political move. Perhaps they perceive that the future will think badly of those who locked us down.

On October 15th, the *LVRJ* mentioned a study done by an Imperial College researcher who claims that early lockdown helped slow virus deaths. The research is conceptually, hopelessly flawed. It postulates a "comparison group" of ten prior years undifferentiated death data and compares them to month/date correlations in the Corona year and says the differences in deaths in the Corona year are caused by Corona alone. They call this "excess mortality." Baloney! What he is measuring is the total effect of Corona deaths plus lockdowns, job loss, and multiple stressors. All this is achieved by not directly measuring the Corona deaths!

13

THE BACK TO SCHOOL
FIGHT HEATS UP
(JULY 9, 10, ETC.)

Nationally, and locally in Nevada, the fight over how and when to send kids back to school heated up suddenly. The local school mogul, Jesus Jara, Superintendent of the Clark County School District, ambitiously proposed that all students, come September, would return to school two days a week and do three days distance learning. Parents had the option to keep their kids physically out of school all five days and just do distance learning.

Mayor Goodman made a personal plea to Jara to make an exemption for grades Pre-K through 5 to be allowed to go to school five days a week with temperature checks administered to children before entering the bus.

Although I am not a pediatrician, I think this plan exemption had strong merit. Children that age need to be nurtured and socialized by contact with human beings, not computers. The plan was not approved.

On the same day Jara made his pitch, the local teachers' union hoisted another ambitious plan which would give parents and teachers a choice. Parents could choose to send their kids to school five days a week or not at all and do distance learning five days a week.

Meanwhile, on the national scene, Dr. Fauci, the icon himself, said it was urgent to get the kids back in school. The head of the CDC, Dr. Redfield, reiterated that the CDC never advised that schools be shut down permanently or on a widespread basis. That is true and I discussed this very point in an earlier section.

On July 10th, Washoe County (Reno) schools unveiled their school plan for September. Elementary school children would go to school five days a week! The others would do mixed or split schedules. Distance learning was also an option.

On July 26th, a Washoe County public health official cancelled those plans. Not because there was a fault in their specific reopening plan but because the county was now deemed in a higher general Corona risk category! A triumph of bureaucratic stupidity of medical bean counters over common sense. The sins (Corona cases) of the father (the county) were to be visited upon the children who had no part in their making. Courageously the Washoe County schools ignored this bureaucrat, and in a September 20th article in the *LVRJ*, they were celebrating completion of their first month of in-person school, dealing not only with Covid-19 but with forest fire smoke.

As I expected, none of the ambitious Clark County plans went anywhere in Las Vegas and all public school kids went into distance learning in September. In the first days of November, the school district sent volunteers out to find kids who were "lost" from distance learning. These were the first electronic truant officers.

It is sad to see what little constructive thought has been given to ways to make school buildings and operations safer for kids when they do return to school. Someone should have been working on this months ago. Are temperature checks of children, teachers, and school staff the only defense schools will have? In my opinion, that is more than enough, especially for children eleven and under.

Perhaps these highly paid school administrators should seek information from the many countries, especially in Scandinavia, that reopened their schools in mid-April or never closed them at all. It's possible there are places here in the US who have quietly and successfully reopened their schools without fanfare. Why doesn't Clark talk to Washoe?

However, since no one is talking much about how to fix schools to make them safe, I would like to toss some ideas out there. These are ideas I have discussed with one of Zack's recent teachers but she wants to remain anonymous for fear of losing her job.

These mixed or blended plans of in-person and distance learning could cut classroom size in half but would that be enough? If prior class size was thirty-eight students, can a half-size classroom of nineteen students be safe? Maybe. Maybe not. We will not know if the kids' higher immunity holds until the kids go back to school.

Teachers could divide their classes into two groups, teaching Group A in the morning and then starting Group B at 11 a.m. By using shortened lesson periods all children will have the discipline of going to school five days a week and will have access to free breakfasts and lunches, which many of them need. This will be hard on teachers, of course, but would not increase the number of hours they work at school. At the same time, a 3 p.m. to 6 p.m. study hall could be organized using substitute teachers to help the kids with their homework or other learning issues. Likely these substitutes could be paid for with 100% of federal emergency corona funds.

This plan would seem to be better than the unpopular two full days a week in school and three off on computer, especially for the elementary grades. It would also deliver the necessary smaller class size, give kids the discipline of going five days a week, and most importantly, have children spend fewer hours indoors on any day they go to school. This will lessen their overall air exposure to enclosed places.

A variant could be to run schools for 16 hours daily with three shifts, affording even smaller classroom numbers. Unless schools start experimenting, they will not know what works best. That requires volunteers and choice.

Some teachers will certainly be brave enough to do their jobs as millions of priority workers have done throughout this pandemic.

Schools are operated differently than other buildings because they are constructed and operated to "full capacity." Most schools have homerooms for older students who then usually travel to other teachers for different subjects. The younger students are in the same classroom all day.

In a business, workers have a desk while factory workers have a workstation. A new configuration could be set up with students having a homeroom desk enclosed with protective plastic side panels and they would wear clear head shields. Teachers could come to the homeroom to deliver lectures on other subjects or students could shift classrooms taking their head shields. Children would get multiple recesses or walkabouts to get them out into the open air, as suggested by Dr. Fauci.

Why do I say new configuration? Older readers will be puzzled by this. Be aware that in teaching, like in most things, there are fashions that go in and out of style. Apparently, in California and some other western states, it is the fashion to have "collaborative" teaching. This means students sit at worktables in little groups facing each other. This teaching configuration is no longer likely to be safe. Teachers may need to go back to the old way of teaching with kids in single desks in rows to allow for proper Covid-19 spacing.

At the end of July, Vice-President Pence gave a last minute pitch for getting kids into five-day, in-person classes in September so their parents could get back to work! Many parents have neither the finances nor family networks to arrange childcare or private school for their children. Clark County government (not the school district) recognized that need and set-up and successfully ran a day camp this summer for kids whose parents could not afford commercial childcare facilities (which were also open and functioning to those who could pay). All without any kids getting Covid-19.

During this Covid-19 summer, a number of in-person classes were successfully taught at UNLV, Nevada State College, NSC in Henderson, and College of Southern Nevada.

Meanwhile, in late August, North Las Vegas government set up a "substitute school" similar to the Clark County Summer Camp called North Las Vegas Southern Nevada Urban Micro Academy. That, and a number of private and parochial schools in town were the only places kids received in-person instruction from live teachers.

Around the Columbus Day/Indigenous Peoples weekend, the *LVRJ* ran an impassioned editorial promoting the reopening of Las Vegas in-person schooling based on pragmatic negotiation between parties.

In reference to the NEA president's belief that 50,000 children will die if the schools are reopened: remember, that is just someone's guestimate, not written on tablets on Mount Sinai. Since only around a hundred children have died so far, that estimate seems inflated to preposterous dimensions. Children on lockdown have played with other children and have been around adults who might have it. Those who have been kept locked away from other children are likely to have mental problems.

Medical staff now speak of children as having first responder immune cells that wane with age. It is nature that is protecting our children, not teachers.

Also, the president of NEA is reacting as if all these deaths would occur all at once, instead of over years, and in one place, maybe her own school district. She probably has not considered Covid-19 might be around for three to four years and failure to reopen our schools will eventually cause the destruction of public education as we know it today; it might even force the removal or retirement of those who stand in the way.

My neighborhood has never decorated much for Halloween but this year they have gone over the top with expensive and creative lighting

displays including 12-foot skeletons. Why? I think people feel bad that kids are not in school and want to do something special for them.
Trick or treat survived but only for those ages two to eight. Parents kept their nine to twelve year-olds home (sadly) and teenagers also (appropriately).

14

ELECTIONS IN LAS VEGAS: THE PRIMARY
AND THE PRESIDENTIAL
(NOVEMBER)

THE PRIMARY

The mid-year voting which took place on June 9th in Las Vegas was not really a traditional primary since presidential choice selection was not a ballot issue there, having been done using caucusing by the individual political parties. Ninety-plus percent of the voting was over local judgeships and state positions. The usual voter turnout for this kind of election was in the 10-20% range.

The Democratic Party sued Clark County beforehand and to settle this dispute the county acceded to the demand that all registered votes be sent a mail-in ballot. Ballots were sent to 1.3 million Nevada voters. Approximately 300,000 mail ballots were returned and accepted. A large number got sent back by the post office for incorrect addresses. As for the rest, people chose not to vote and assumedly those unused ballots ended either in recycle bins or trash cans.

Because of strong local demand by voters, the county opened three in-person voting sites for the entire county. On June 9th, all three locations were swamped with voters, many of them waiting hours to vote.

The Democrats, in their lawsuit against the county had also suggested the county forego its usual voter signature confirmation process of verifying with the signature on file. This would, the Democrats said, save money and increase voter participation. The county refused and confirmed all signatures.

In planning for the presidential election, the Democrats finally accepted that mail-in ballots should only be sent to "active" voters whose addresses were more likely to be up-to-date. Remember, one million mail-in votes were thrown away in the primary.

Historically, Nevadans have done ninety percent of their voting in person. In August, Nevada's Secretary of State Barbara Cegavske, unveiled her simple and inexpensive plan: All usual in-person voting sites would be open for early voting and on election day. Anyone who wanted a mail/absentee ballot could get one for the asking with no reason necessary. Previously, to get a mail-in/absentee ballot you had to have a reason (infirmity, distance, etc.); however, this rule was dropped early on.

Democrats in Carson City tossed out this simple plan in favor of an expensive plan that sent all active voters a mail-in ballot whether they wanted one or not. Voters did not have to use the ballot and could vote early in person or on election day at a polling place. There were no restrictions on ballot collecting or "harvesting," and automatic un-postmarked mail-in ballots were authenticated for three days after election day. The process for counting mail-in ballots in Nevada could last until the ninth day after the election if needed.

Vote harvesting or collecting ballots of any kind used to be illegal in Nevada. Republicans believed that was a protection against voter harassment and hustling, and potential ballot abuse. In recent years, Democrats won an exemption for "in-family vote collecting." Perhaps that was just a steppingstone towards their newly achieved goal.

Many states do not regularly prune their voting rolls thus creating more "loose" mail ballots. A watchdog organization called Judicial Watch sues such offenders.

There are aspects of Nevada's new mail-in vote rejection routines which I believe are patently unfair on their face and any court would surely find fault with them particularly their rule (bragged about in an article in the *LVRJ*) about how one ballot envelope received with two ballots enclosed from the same address are both automatically disqualified. Frugal old married couples might see no sense in costing the county extra postage by sending their ballots in separately. Should they lose their right to vote for the president? Unjustifiable!

Other issues include confusing or contradictory language about signature verification and safeguards, and the collection of multiple ballots; lawyers and columnists are in dire disagreement before the show even begins. That is an invitation to litigation.

Mail-in ballots in the primary required full signatures on the outside of the envelope. As has been pointed out in the past (*LVRJ* letters to the editor) this sets up the voter for identity theft! A serious defect of the rushed mid-year voting plan and one that should have been fixed and was not. It does not help that Las Vegas readers were treated to the news in October of a local postal carrier being accused of unemployment fraud and a postal worker fired in Louisville over 110 unopened mail ballots in a dumpster.

Under this new voting plan, I worry that vote stealing is possible. Anyone can simply alter a mail-in ballot by crossing out the first entry and checking their new selection. No initials or signature needed. Too easy!

That makes a mail-in ballot an instantly negotiable instrument, perfect for vote stealing and selling. Large scale mail voting is inherently less secure than in-person voting.

By mid-August, Cegavske's plan for opening all in-person voting sites had been compromised by the dropping of 25 or so sites. This forced many people who planned to vote in person to have to choose between waiting a long time in voting lines or using the less well preferred mail option.

I would not be surprised if 50-60% of Las Vegas voters still go to the polls. That would be a repudiation of the Carson City plan. If such a statistic was reported, I did not see it.

In retrospect, I believe voting in Nevada was handled honestly and competently but I still believe mail-in balloting is problematic and after the pandemic we should return to the prior status quo.

The "Save Trump" legal initiatives, which were rightfully doomed to failure as even their legal staffs knew early on, can still be useful for locating weak spots in our voting systems. The Nevada one claimed it did a match (with nearly 4,000 hits) comparing voters and resident aliens with no eligibility to vote. That is worth looking at to see if it was done correctly! Every newly-licensed Nevada driver is automatically registered to vote. Yet some kinds of licenses are issued to non-citizens and there have been known slip-ups.

Computer matching has been a tool for identifying fraud since the eighties. Failure to use it is a political decision.

15

LAS VEGAS TALL TALE: HOW I BOT DE PRESIDENT AND MADE A BUNDLE (NOVEMBER 4) BY SALLY "DE SCRIBE" SICILIANO

I'm a Vegas guy from way back. My mob has been around town since the sixties. Yestaday I cleared $500k on a business caper selling mail ballots to da side dat think it won de election. Here's de story behine my brag.

I first got ideas when I noticed one million mail ballots what got trashcanned in de primary. My nose tell me dere was money to be made here somewhere. When de new rules of AB 4 come, I knew we was on a hot trail. When de politicians and de lawyers start fussing bout what de law mean, den you know you got a sweet thing workin for ya in my business. I'm like an adventure capitalist ya might say.

See, what I dun first is enlis a bunch of guys and dolls ta collect a whole bunch of dem mail ballots. Didn't matter if dey has signatures already or writin on dem. They could all be fixed up. Da people dat goes out and hunts up ballots is da same ones dat would fix dose dat needed fixin later.

De word wasto hit the big apartment houses and snag any loose ballots before the postman took dem back. Den to check the blue bins where dey recycle paper and de trash cans.

We tried us some moles in da voting places to snag them drop boxes and in de post office but we come up short dis time. We be back!

I hire both de pros and de punks and give them $3 a ballot. Young punks will hustle for ya. De pros I need for later for de tricky stuff. I also says they all can go door to door and offer to hep people with her ballots and deliver their ballots to de county ballot drop boxes so's they don't get delayed in da mail. Dis fear of the slow-top mailman done give us a bundle extra.

When we wasn't getting enuf ballots I sent my pros out to de homeless shelters and get people registered to vote and paid dem $5 for de ballot and $2 to my pro. Some of my best grifters I sends out to buy ballots from poor folk door to door. De best line they is to use is "I never got my mail ballot cause I moved. Can you sell me yours for $5? You can always request another one or vote in person."

One of my crazy Tex-Mex pros come up with his own smooth gig. He knew a bunch of wetbacks in his hood and talked them into registering to vote by computer under phony names, and when their papers come, he scooped der mail ballots for $3 a pop. Dey thot he was Santa Claus but he was Pancho Villa.

As de mail ballots come in, dey is all numbered and my computer jockey builds a "scoresheet" like in baseball; he lists each ballot and feeds it ina master list. A ballet what comes fresh, signed and untouched from da voter we call a "virgin." A ballot what needs fixin we call a "hot potato." A ballot that comes untouched and unsigned is a mule, what needs help from a scribbler to get ina da horse race. As we collects and stores dese ballots, we run copies of da voter signatures on de outside of de envelope and sells dese to an autograph collector what works in credit cards.

When we harvest 20,000 of these babies we sen all de candidates and de two parties a e-mail message what can't be traced and tole them we was selling votes and we be in touch.

At noon on Election Day, we had 41,320 ballots in hand. De east coast voting early returns show near even steven for da president. We tell both parties "first come, first serve." Forty-one thousand votes is for sale for $15 each. From da $619,800 we was to pay off our people and the $500k is cream for de pussycat. Meow! If no one buys we tells them we is dumping all de votes for dat Liberation party broad.

If we paid our cash by 3:00 p.m. all ballots was to be distributed within three hours to over a hunnerd vote drop boxes at all voting locations in de county.

Well, dem slackers in suits was late. At 3:57 p.m. we sends the word to move em out. Since all the voting locations was swamped we got all drop-offs done before closing time. A deal is a deal!
We made a little on some of the small potatoes candidates but them an other details is slippin fast outa my mind. It sure was a lot of fun. That Mr. Barnum was right. Maybe we play this game again some day! See ya round, sports!

16

WHEN WILL THE PANDEMIC END?
WHAT WILL BE THE FINAL DEATH TOLL?
(DECEMBER)

First estimates by the early optimists were that the end of the summer of 2020 the Covid-19 pandemic would be over. The pessimists, at that time, said a second wave might hit us in the fall of 2020, mixing with the seasonality of the flu. Some people even thought Covid-19 would come back in 2021.

It looks to me they are all wrong. It looks like Covid-19 comes in alternating waves but is more or less continuously here, there, and everywhere. It might even be around for years to come. Why should it not try to access all eight billion of us? What will stop it?

Corona seems to closely resemble the Spanish Flu of 1917, 1918, and 1919. It took two to three years for the Spanish Flu to infect everyone in the world. After the first few weeks and months when people were most scared, society did not shut down to hide but went on, business as usual.

Since we have systematically tried to protect some populations such as children (the least vulnerable) and the elderly, it is likely to take longer this time around. I remember Fauci recently saying it could last for one to two more years. It looks like three to four year to me. I will go on record predicting the end of the pandemic on February 29, 2024 (Sadie Hawkins Day). Ladies, carpe diem. There will be fewer males around then! Of course, by the end of 2023 things may be back to normal so we might consider Sadie Hawkins Day as the ceremonial end to this pestilence.

I cannot help feeling like General Kitchener did at the beginning of World War I when asked how many more weeks the war would last (and everyone believed it would soon end). He said, "Three years." Everyone took him for senile until history proved even his estimate (which was the best) was far short of the mark.

Playing hide and go seek may delay your getting it and if you are super careful and lucky maybe you will not get it at all. Maybe your immune system will be so strong it will not even know it has been attacked.

For clarity's sake, I repeat that I count the beginning of the US's pandemic as January 1, 2020. China and the world pandemic I clock as having started September 1, 2019. I do not see the election of a new US president on November 8th affecting either the trajectory or duration of the epidemic. Nevada's clock pretty much started on March 1st.

On October 6th, WHO threw out the blockbuster assertion, based on its review of antibody studies, that ten percent of the world's population (760 million) already had Corona. It is possible! It has taken only thirteen months to get this far so in two or three more years it ought to have reached everywhere on the planet. Under this alternative view of reality, continuation of lockdowns looks suicidal.

You are probably wondering why I used thirteen months in the previous paragraph. I have always suspected Covid-19 began in September 2019 in Wuhan, China and on October 18, 2020, I saw an article in the Epoch Times (a new newspaper in my neighborhood grocery store) that published a credible report of treatment of multiple cases of a Covid-like disease in Wuhan in October 2019 and one reported the month before!

These dates suggest another possiblity; it all began in Wuhan and the Chinese were careless. Maybe even their military.

Let us do some rough numbers. The US death toll hit 331,902 as of 7 p.m. PDT on December 26, 2020. If you divide 332,000 by 12 months you get a monthly death rate of approximately 28,000. Currently the death rate is running closer to 2,000 monthly rather than 1,000. This issue will be addressed presently.

Of course, effective vaccines could theoretically drop the death rate by half. Choose your number like in a bingo game. There is very little SCIENCE knows about this bug's future and even current behavior. Many theories but few certainties. We will need to see, post vaccines, where the numbers in the death rate go.

Dr. Fauci even said some time ago that we would be lucky to get a vaccine with 50% effectiveness. Pfizer says its vaccine is 95% effective! Moderna's is 94.5% effective.

If you assume your vaccine is 50% effective you might believe that automatically means a lowering of the death rate by half but the real world does not work that way. Probably there will be a reduction, by how much is total guesswork. The 50% of people for whom the vaccine works would not get Covid-19. The unprotected group and the unvaccinated could theoretically be where all the deaths occur. Yet that same scenario is possible with vaccines with 95% effectiveness! We cannot identify in advance those people for whom the virus will be fatal.

Using the most optimistic of all these assumptions that the vaccines will cut the death rate by 95%, it is possible that by September 2021 or as soon as the vaccines become widely distributed, the death rate might drop to only 1,400 per month.

We have been discussing the "effectiveness" ratings of vaccines. We mentioned Pfizer at 95% and Moderna at 94.5%. More accurately, these are "efficacy" ratings applied to studies under laboratory conditions. After months of study following the administration of vaccines to people in the real world, true "effectiveness" ratings for each vaccine will be developed. These numbers are generally lower than efficacy ratings.

For the sake of explication, let us assume that all Americans get inoculated with vaccines rated as 95% effective.

Under the most pessimistic assumptions it is possible the US death rate will not drop at all! How is that possible? It is possible the people now dying from Covid-19 are in the same "five percent pool" for whom the vaccines will not work.

Is there room for this overlap? Yes, there is. The number now dying is only a fraction of one percent of the population. The number the vaccines would not work on is five percent of our population, which is approximately 16½ million people.

Is there a likelihood to be a perfect overlap of "fatally susceptible" and "vaccine failures?" This is pure conjecture but intuitively I feel there has to be some overlap. There certainly is a pool of medically fragile and susceptible people in our population. We do not know why some peoples' immune systems go rogue on them and start attacking their own body's defenses. Why some people (mostly men) die while apparently similar patients live. A dangerous mystery.

Clearly, there are some hidden medical factors besides the obvious ones such as age, high blood pressure, diabetes, etc.) which make some people fatally susceptible to Covid-19. There may be multiple reasons these people are dying or possibly just a few.

At last some fruitful findings are beginning to emerge. Under a Kaiser Health News research summary (*LVRJ* November 2020), scientists are looking at the presence of auto-antibodies which disable key immune system proteins called interferons as well as mutations in genes that control the interferons involved in fighting viruses. Another promising area is inhaled interferon therapy.

A solution to the dilemma of our medically fragile and susceptible people does not appear likely in the near future. We may need to closely monitor the death rate to see if the Pfizer vaccine and the Moderna vaccine have a noticeably positive effect upon it. Hopefully, this will be the case.

A field biologist friend of mine, Wolfgang Coldren, has a whole different outlook on all this. He says Corona is just Mother Nature's way of "cleaning house." He told me, "We are a part of nature and the weak in any species are the favored prey of the carnivore. Corona is our current biologic carnivore. Wolves, for example, do not choose the strong, healthy elk; they look for the old, the injured, the sick and the weak or the very young and stupid. Sickness often comes from environmental sources such as overpopulation or destruction of habitat. Maybe Mother Nature is telling us eight billion people on the planet is too many."

What can we learn from the Corona experience that would help us deal better with future epidemics? Perhaps that lockdowns are not the answer and that strong public health infrastructure is important, and all young people should be taught early on the basics of biology and health education.

Dr. Coldren also left me with some interesting thoughts. "The winners post-Corona will be the medical insurance companies and the medical establishment itself because Corona will have killed off the sickest of the sick and many chronically ill. This will leave room for the reduction of the overall cost of medical care or an uptake in profit-taking, depending on who acts first. Or it could be an opportunity to vastly expand Medicaid, perhaps even under the aegis of public health operations."

Dr. Fauci also thinks young people are being careless about Corona and that is helping the surge of cases. Maybe he is right and maybe they are right not to care. They may be doing us a favor. One could argue that the controversial restriction against crowds and big groups of people do nothing but extend the length of the epidemic, holding back the reaching of "herd immunity." That issue needs to be looked at for the sake of future policy.

Some countries such as the US, Italy, UK, and Sweden have been chided for their slowness in closing down and instituting home arrest. As of July 7th, per Johns Hopkins, the Covid-19 death rate per 100,000 people is 42, 58, 68, and 55 respectively. There are other low-rate countries like China with a not to be believed .33 rate, and South Korea with .57. It is claimed that all of these countries are using the same techniques to fight infections.

Why the difference? It has got to be mostly in the characteristics of the different populations. For example, Italy is known to have had many fragile elderly. In August, a new factor—obesity—has been identified as high risk for Covid-19 to the extent that obese people do not respond well to vaccines. America has a pre-existing obesity problem which could be exacerbated by the pandemic. My proof? Look at ice cream consumption figures.

It may also be that many governments have political reasons for not wanting to show high numbers of cases. It also may be that differences exist in how different countries collect records. We discovered somewhere along the line that China had not been tallying symptom-less patients even though their tests were positive.

I would even conjecture that in the Third World, those countries that did nothing at all about Corona might even be better off than those who did the wrong things. (I discussed this point in a previous chapter.)

Can we honestly say the pandemic is over if international quarantines and travel restriction are still in place? Or more importantly, internal US restrictions that interfere with interstate commerce and the right of US citizens to visit their families in states other than those in which they reside? These rules hurt our economic and social recovery. It is within the president's power to invalidate all the governors' edicts which impede those citizens' constitutional rights. Every American has a right under the US Constitution to freely visit any state or make their home wherever they wish.

Continuing with these quarantine policies may likely create hidden pools of infection that will come back to bite us later.

Also, the epidemic "isn't over til the fat lady sings." That is when most people feel safe to go back to the opera, to an indoor restaurant, to a rock concert, or a movie. That will come some time after lockdowns and masks go away.

Aside from the socio-medical issues, the near shutdown of the world's economic system over Covid can't help but have messed up our future. Will we see a recession, or something insidiously worse? Some things may never be the same again.

ASSORTED ISSUES RELATED TO EPIDEMIC'S END

Year End Surge

As the year comes to its end, Corona cases are surging higher in Nevada. The death toll on December 31, 2020 was 59, the highest ever.

That did not keep my neighborhood from its traditional ritual of setting off fireworks for the last fifteen minutes of 2020 (with fireworks they kept from their July 4th purchases).

Nor did it keep the young people on the Strip from seeing in the New Year while Times Square stood empty. Bravo Las Vegas! The human spirit needs occasional congregate celebration despite the risk. Some people call this Corona Year "annus horribilis."

Will this current wave continue upward? Hard to tell at this point. The numbers are zigzagging, probably due to the holidays.

Covid-19 seems to come in vaguely defined waves of 5-6 months. It is unclear whether we are still in the ascending part of the wave or on the descending side. If we are on the descending portion, we will probably see a drop in January and February with a massive new, larger wave starting upward in March. If the timing is right, the widespread availability of vaccines by then might blunt that wave at its end in June.

New Variants

New variants of Corona have popped up recently in Britain, South Africa, Nigeria, Colorado, and California. Are these of concern? Probably not. Some time ago scientists studied an earlier variant known as 614g. This mutation of the Covid virus had become more contagious but appeared the same in lethality. Viruses often mutate but it is likely the vaccine already developed will work on all these new strains (of which the US has six at year's end). New—and more contagious—strains will surely appear. Claims for their increased lethality should be suspect. Even medical workers can get hysterical.

Medical After-Effects of Covid-19

A number of people have suffered relapses (or new cases?) of Covid-19. A number of people have multiple medical impediments post Covid, including brain fog and memory problems. If these persist and worsen they could result in future severe medical handicaps.

The newest development in this area is the appearance of severe psychotic symptoms in persons with no prior history of mental impairment, including paranoid and potentially homicidal ideation. These bizarre manifestations came after the person(s) had just recovered from Covid-19. The anti-psychotic risperidone has been useful in a number of cases. Persistent immune activation (where the immune system cannot shut down or is confused) is considered a likely cause.

Aside from these rare and exotic manifestations, the future holds a tidal wave of PTSD-Corona cases, including school children, that will surely swamp the mental health system.

Viral Load

When a PCR test is performed to determine if someone has Covid, it is performed in steps or cycles. In the first cycle a small amount of the patient's genetic material is examined. If a "positive" is obtained right away, the person has a low cycle threshold or "Ct" and a high viral load. If no positive is obtained, the amount of genetic material is doubled (at each additional cycle).

In one study, as reported by Apoorva Mandavilli of the *New York Times*, in the *Las Vegas Desert Sun (LVDS)* of January 1, 2021, "The Nevada Department of Public Health found an average Ct value of 23.4 in people who died from Covid-19, compared with 27.5 in those who survived their illness. People who were asymptomatic had an average value of 29.6 suggesting they carried much less virus than the other two groups."

The information on Ct levels is generally available when a PCR test is processed but has not been reported routinely.

Some people exposed to lots of virus never seem to get it. It is conjectured they have a natural immunity. Some people (a tiny number) seem to have a natural immunity to some other diseases. Unfortunately, there is no safe way to determine if you are immune. Get a vaccine!

This is an area of medicine I am not knowledgeable about. For example, are all people with immunity to some disease also "carriers" for that disease? Or are there immunes who are not carriers? This becomes an important issue when we talk next about "The Phantom Menace."
Is There a Phantom Menace?

This phantom issue continues to haunt serious discussion of Covid-19. In an Associated Press article in the *LVRJ* on December 12, 2020, the authors say, "No one yet knows whether it (the vaccine) can stop the silent, symptomless spread that accounts for roughly half of all cases."

Where did this new Golem come from? Last I heard the (unfounded) assertion by the CDC was that 35% of Covid-19 cases were "silent spreaders." Where is the proof of the existence of so many phantoms? Half of all cases is preposterous!

The article further states, "The ongoing study will attempt to answer that..."

And how will the Pfizer study identify silent spreaders? It has no protocol to do so. Vaccine studies were "Specifically designed to see whether vaccines protect people from getting sick from Covid-19. If volunteers developed symptoms like a fever or cough, they were then tested for the Corona virus." The quote is from an earlier vaccine article in the *LVDS* on November 22, 2020 by Carl Zimmer (*New York Times*) who also says, "We don't have answers yet to whether vaccinated people can get asymptomatic infections..."

It looks to me like the Associated Press folk are hoping someone is studying the issue, and I join them in that desire but I do not see it coming from the vaccine studies.

As I said earlier in the narrative, I agree with WHO's assertion that the number of symptomless cases is very small. I believe in this issue the CDC has gotten off trail.

Maybe the Chinese were right early in 2020 after all, not to count as

Covid-19 cases those very few that tested positive who insisted they had no symptoms. Maybe these are "carriers" (people who can pass on the disease but do not themselves get sick from it). Another possibility is that they are people who tested positive but had a low viral load and therefore not as likely to pass on the disease to other people. A third possibility is that these symptomless people do not continue in this condition for long, and either get better, or worse! In short, this could be a normal development stage of the disease where a person's immune system is fighting off the Corona invaders. A win or loss is likely—a permanent stasis is highly unlikely.

The Chinese seem to be the only ones trying to measure the incidence of the "phantoms." A recurrence of Corona in the Chinese cities of Shijiazhuang and Xingtai in Hebei province produced a count of "197 people without symptoms who tested positive" (*LVRJ* January 10, 2021). This count is still kept separate from regular Covid-19 stats and looks to me like it backs up WHO's assertions.

The most logical probability is that a vaccine would be able to kill a symptomless spreader (ss) because a "ss" looks like a person with a low viral load. The least likely scenario is that a vaccine would be unable to "fix" a symptomless spreader. Reality has its own logic so I accept the hypothetical possibility that vaccines cannot fix a "ss" (whatever that is).

This is in the area of speculation of what is the worst that can happen? Like my earlier speculation on the death rate and coverage of those who are "fatally susceptible." Let us hope all of the speculations are proven wrong by time.

Vaccination: Who First? And How?

Even at the end of 2020, it looks like the vaccination process is shaping up to be an unhappy and inefficient disaster.

To save the most American lives, those who are at most risk of dying from Covid-19 (those who daily treat Covid-19 patients and seniors 75 years of age and over) should have been first.

The vaccine should have been given directly to the medical insurance providers and/or pharmacies of the elderly (under Medicare and Social Security). Why set up a circus-like (even with reservations) mass vaccination system as is shaping up in Nevada. My 90-year-old neighbor who uses a walker and has no access to a computer, cannot wait in line with spry 70-year-olds or 25-year old teachers, and therefore has to wait longer for a vaccine. Is it too much to ask that an elderly person receive their vaccinations from their doctor or as is the case in West Virginia, from their pharmacists?

Can the Pandemic be Tamed?

The miraculous development of at least two vaccines with 95% efficiency means control of this pandemic is now theoretically possible, though there will be many logistical and social problems still ahead. We won't see the end of Covid for at least three more years globally for various reasons, including vaccine resistance, Third World supply problems, and our failure to recognize the predictable "wave" nature (5-6 months) of Covid.

It has periods of low activity interspersed with bursts of high activity and contagion, mistakenly labeled as "surges" by the press. Surges are erratic and unpredictable. The Covid bugs are living entities; this is their life rhythm.

The 4th wave is likely to peak next summer and cause the usual hysterical panic. We are likely to see the 5th and 6th waves too. Covid will keep coming back until most everyone has gotten vaccinated, gotten immunity by illness or natural immunity, or died.

Future Hysteria?

One of the things that will fuel future (needless) panic is when vaccinated people start coming down with Covid. This is to be expected even with two vaccines given a 95% rating. No vaccine is 100% effective.

CDC record keeping should enable them to spot when this "donut hole" gets bigger than 5%, perhaps signaling a reduction of the efficiency of the primary vaccines.

What will bureaucrats and medical workers do during future hysteria attacks? Order people to wear masks of course. Since I doubt schools will open before September, I hope they don't lay this burden on children, especially young ones. That would be, psychologically speaking, a terrorist act. Of course in Wuhan the government would just test all eleven million people yet again.

Future hysterical outbursts will come as attacks on those who refuse vaccination. People will be threatened with losing their jobs if they don't "vac." The result of such mandates will be social turmoil, ending in the Supreme Court.

Epidemics on Screen

Interested in the best cinematic depictions of epidemics? Try these:

The Andromeda Strain (1971)
Cassandra Crossing (1977)
12 Monkeys (1995)
Outbreak (1995)

Cheer up everyone. The human race has survived far worse! Circle (when you can) the next Sadie Hawkins Day (February 29, 2024) on your calendar.

www.ingramcontent.com/pod-product-compliance
Lightning Source LLC
Chambersburg PA
CBHW011942050726
47590CB00011B/3330